THE MIDNIGHT TRAIN HOME

ERIKA TAMAR

Alfred A. Knopf
New York

Also by Erika Tamar

The Junkyard Dog
Winner of the California Young Reader Medal

In memory of my parents

THIS IS A BORZOI BOOK PUBLISHED BY ALFRED A. KNOPF

Copyright © 2000 by Erika Tamar

"There'll Be Some Changes Made" by Billy Higgins and W. Benton Overstreet used
by permission of EDWARD B. MARKS MUSIC COMPANY

www.randomhouse.com/kids

Library of Congress Cataloging-in-Publication Data

Tamar, Erika.
The midnight train home / Erika Tamar. — 1st ed.
p.   cm.
Summary: When their mother can no longer care for them, eleven-year-old Deirdre
and her brothers board the Orphans' Train for placement with families out West, but Deirdre,
a talented singer, finds a different type of family when she joins a traveling vaudeville troupe.
Includes a note on the Children's Aid Society which operated the orphan trains from 1854 - 1930.

ISBN 0-375-80159-6 (trade) — ISBN 0-375-90159-0 (lib. bdg.)

[1. Orphan trains—Fiction. 2. Brothers and sisters—Fiction.
3. Vaudeville—Fiction. 4. Performing arts—Fiction.] I. Title.
PZ7.T159 Mi 2000
[Fic]—dc21
00-020355

Printed in the United States of America

10   9   8   7   6   5   4   3   2   1

May 2000   First Edition

ONE

Deirdre moved like a sleepwalker, as hollow as if someone had scooped out the inside of her heart. Grand Central Terminal was so big. Track numbers and gates, and stairs to go down. People going every which way. She walked close to her older brother, Sean, so close that sometimes she bumped him. She felt small and lost, and she clutched her little brother Jimmy's hand too hard as the agent hurried them along with the group. Jimmy squirmed and whimpered, so she loosened her grip. Her other hand held tight around the handle of the small cardboard suitcase. O'ROURKE, DEIRDRE was printed on its side in black crayon. Cardboard tags hung over their chests: *Deirdre O'Rourke, Age 11. Sean O'Rourke, Age 13. James O'Rourke, Age 3.*

There were eighty other kids with them—little ones like Jimmy, others bigger than Sean, all of them in fresh-starched clothes, all of them carrying cardboard suitcases with their names in black crayon. Some of the kids were unruly and noisy. A quiet group walked automatically in double file; the girls wore the same navy pinafores, the boys had the same blue shirts. They had to be from the orphanage, Deirdre thought. And for a moment she was grateful the new dress she'd been given was different, with brown and white checks.

Before yesterday, she'd never even heard of the Children's Aid Society; she hadn't known anything about trains taking city kids to someplace far away. Not until Mum had handed each of them a suitcase from Children's Aid. Yesterday. August 23, 1927. At least the date was something real to hold on to.

A loudspeaker blared. "Track Four. Washington… Richmond…"

Mum had to have planned this way before yesterday. When? Why?

The loudspeaker voice echoed in Deirdre's mind. "Richmond…Richmond…"

Deirdre pulled Jimmy along and looked up at Sean. "Did you know?" She swallowed the sudden thickness in her throat. "Did Mum tell you ahead of time?"

"No." Sean's lips were set in such a tight line that there was a circle of white around them.

"Last night—you should've stopped her—"

Sean was Mum's favorite; he always got into lots of scrapes, but no matter how good Deirdre behaved, Sean was still her favorite. He could have—

"She had it all set," he said. "All your hollering and crying didn't change anything. You were just making her feel worse."

Making Mum feel worse! When had Sean said that before?—something like that, long ago. She could almost remember…

It was all she could do to make Jimmy keep up. He was only three; he couldn't walk that fast. Anyway, he wasn't used to wearing shoes.

A gate. A sign: TRACK 9. Jimmy held on to the banister; he was slow on the stairs. The platform was dimly lit. Everything was gray. A train with a long line of cars stretched as far as Deirdre could see. There was smoke rising, and hissing and rumbling.

"Here we are," the lady agent said.

Deirdre hadn't known the word *agent* before. Mum explained, "They're the ones from Children's Aid taking care of you while you're traveling. So you see, it'll be fine." As if anything could be fine again!

The lady agent had come for them early that morning; she found them in front of the building on Division Street. She had bobbed hair and wore a cloche. Deirdre could tell she was the uptown kind.

When the lady came to get them, all Mum had said was, "Remember to say your prayers." She'd wiped a smudge from Deirdre's cheek. "Be good."

"No! No, Mum, I don't want—"

"Sure it's grand and glorious places you'll go, all the way west." Mum had put on a pretend smile, but her voice was a whisper. Deirdre could hardly hear her over the rumble of an ice truck driving by.

The lady had glanced at their blanket spread out on the sidewalk and quickly looked away. The lady *knew* they were living out on the street, 'cause that's where she came to get them, Deirdre thought. So why did she have to look so embarrassed and shame them?

Mum had handed Sean an envelope. "Here's the address I'll be at. Send me a word about how you're doing." Sean had nodded and tucked the envelope deep inside the pocket of his knickers.

If Mum had an address, she'd found someplace to live. So why was she sending them away? She didn't love them at all, not at all, none of them, not even Sean.

When it was time for them to go, Mum had abruptly turned. She walked stiff-legged and fast down the street, with her arms wrapped tight around her body. Deirdre watched her back until she disappeared into the crowd on the corner.

No good-bye, no hug, nothing.

At Children's Aid, Jimmy and Sean were led away with some other boys, and Deirdre had yelled and struggled until the agents promised it was just for the bath. That whole morning was a blur. Getting scrubbed in a real bathtub, the lady combing her hair, the smell of disinfectant, a brand-new dress and one extra to keep in the suitcase. When she was reunited with Sean, he suddenly looked thin and gangly, his collarbones sticking out from a too-big white shirt.

The kids on the station platform were all over the place, waiting, restless. Deirdre let herself be jostled. She held the handle of the suitcase tight; her nails dug into her palm.

There was someone's father—he looked like an old rummy, red nose like the men at Gallagher's. He was crying, and a little boy was hanging on to his leg.

Mum could have come.

Except for the rummy, there were no other parents. 'Cause these kids are orphans, Deirdre thought. Not like us. This was the orphans' train. It wasn't right!

The doors opened with a *whoosh*. The agents herded them onto the train. Deirdre was pushed along with the flow.

"Wait!" Sean stopped short beside her. "I lost it!"

"What?"

"I forgot, the hole in my pocket!" Sean snaked through the rush of kids getting on. "I lost it!"

Deirdre, hanging on to Jimmy, frantically struggled to follow him. She couldn't let Sean out of her sight!

"What's the problem here?" an agent asked.

"I gotta go back and find it," Sean said. "I lost my mum's address!"

"That's okay," the man agent said. "You won't need it where you're going."

Sean made a move to shove the man out of his way.

The agent grabbed Sean's arms and held them down. "Easy, now," he said.

The hopelessness of finding one little scrap of envelope somewhere in the city washed over Sean's face. He let the agent lead them back.

They boarded the train.

TWO

They'd never been on a train before. Any other time, they would have been excited, Deirdre thought. Well, Jimmy was; he looked around with big eyes and kept repeating "choo-choo." He didn't understand what was happening to them. Not that she understood, not really, not the why of it.

They sat where the agent pointed. Deirdre took the window seat, and Jimmy curled next to her. Sean faced them from the window seat directly across.

A boy with bad cross-eyes was put in the aisle seat next to Sean. His name tag was turned the wrong way. He was skinny and small, and at first Deirdre guessed that he was ten. When she looked more carefully, she saw that he had an old face.

Kids filled every seat in the car.

"I just stuck it in my pocket," Sean said. "I never even looked at the address."

For a moment, Sean's face was raw with hurt. Deirdre

looked away. She trailed her fingers along the window glass.

"If Mum found a place to stay at, how come she didn't take us?" Deirdre asked. "She could've taken us there with her."

"Could be a bad place. Someplace she couldn't bring us."

The seat was dark green plush, prickly against Deirdre's legs.

"There's nothing that bad," she said.

"Yeah, there is. The TB ward at the hospital. Big Polly's house with her ladies. Plenty places kids can't go."

Sean had his face back to no expression at all, no sign of anything except for his clenched fists with the knuckles turning white. "Listen, I don't know."

"Big Polly's nice to me. She gives me pennies."

"You don't understand about her," Sean said harshly.

"I do, too! But anyplace is better than out on the street. Isn't it?"

Sean didn't answer.

"Well, isn't it?"

They'd been living on the street all of last week. Deirdre couldn't blame Mrs. Monahan that much for turning them out of her basement room on Division Street. It was too crowded, what with the five Monahan kids—Deirdre hated that pushy oldest one, that Bridget Monahan! And then Mum got way behind in her share of the rent, so Mrs. Monahan was bringing other people in. They'd never lived out on the street before. Sean kept saying the luck of the Irish was with them 'cause it wasn't raining, was it?—just to make Mum feel better. Anyway, they snuck into the building to use the toilet in the second-floor hall.

She wished they could have stayed on Rivington Street. That's where they had a room all their own. Rivington Street was back before Jimmy was born, four places before the Monahans', and the best place they'd been; they didn't have to share it with strangers. She wished they could go back there right now.

The train began to move, shaking and chugging. They were still on the underground track. Out the window everything looked dark.

"Where's it gonna stop?" Deirdre asked.

"All different towns. Going west." Sean shrugged. "I don't know."

"Pennsylvania, Indiana, Kansas, ends up in Texas." The cross-eyed kid was breaking right into their conversation as if he knew them. "All along the route, there'll be these nice families waiting for us."

Deirdre couldn't look straight at him for long. It made her feel as if her eyes were crossing, too.

He went prattling on and on. "There'll be farms and animals. Like ducks and horses and cows and chickens and—"

"Where's chickies?" Jimmy climbed over Deirdre's lap toward the black hole of the window.

"—and pigs and roosters and..." the boy continued. He

sounded as if he was repeating every word of a speech that somebody had made to him.

Mum had said some of the same stuff that last night; it must have come straight from the agent. As if the names of a load of farm animals made everything wonderful.

The train was moving aboveground now. The window was sooty. A part of the city that she'd never been in went blurring past.

"Where's chickies?" Jimmy said again.

"No chickies." Deirdre pushed him back into his seat.

The kid continued. "It's good. We get real families and—"

"We have a real family," Deirdre said.

"No, you don't, 'cause you're on the orphans' train."

"We ain't orphans! We got a mum!" Deirdre said.

"She must've signed you over to Children's Aid."

"Why don'tcha shut up and mind your own business?" Sean snarled.

The kid shrugged. "I'm just saying."

If only I'd made more money, Deirdre thought. She'd gone out singing every night; she got plenty of pennies, and nickels, too. She felt proud when folks stopped on the street to listen to her songs. "April Showers." "There's a Little Bit of Heaven, Sure They Called It Ireland." "I Found a Million-Dollar Baby in a Five-and-Ten-Cent Store." "Bye, Bye, Blackbird." Once a man even threw a half-dollar! She should have stayed longer outside Gallagher's speakeasy last Friday night. Friday night was best; that's when the men got their pay. "Danny Boy" was about leaving Ireland forever, and late night, when the men were feeling boozy and soft, that one made the coins ring down. That and "Amazing Grace." But it had been so hot and muggy, and she'd gotten tired.

Sean made lots of money selling the *Daily Mirror,* until the cops got after him for yelling out fake headlines. "Extra! Extra! Jimmy Walker Gunned Down in City Hall!" That was an exciting one, 'cause people liked the fun-loving mayor. Or, "Read all about it, President Coolidge Caught in Love Nest!" Just imagine, Silent Cal! Everybody would rush to buy the paper, and Sean would disappear, quick, before they got to reading it.

Sometimes the true headlines were as crazy as anything Sean could make up. Like Aimee Semple McPherson, the famous evangelist, disappearing. And then turning up in Arizona a month later. It was a fake kidnapping; people whispered she'd been in a love nest all that time, and didn't she look like an angel!

Headlines often said "love nest." Deirdre knew what that really meant, but she imagined a big round nest, cozy and warm with soft feather lining, where a mum would tuck you in and love you forever.

"I hope somebody takes me, first stop." The cross-eyed boy's voice jarred her back to here and now. "The little kids always get picked first. I don't get why everybody wants babies, messing their pants and all." He kept talking, and Deirdre wished he'd quit. "People just like babies, I guess. Your little brother over there—I bet he gets picked first thing."

Deirdre felt a sudden stabbing cold, everything inside her turning into icicles.

"The same people gotta take all of us, don't they?" she asked Sean. "You, me, and Jimmy?"

Sean's eyes widened as if he'd been startled. They were very blue. "I don't know."

She was thinking fast. "Who was Jimmy's da?"

His lips twisted. "Mum never said. You know that."

"Yeah, so Jimmy *could* have the same da as us."

"No. Ours took off way before."

"I know, but—we'll say he's got the same da, okay? So he's got to stay with us?"

Sean didn't answer for a long time.

"No one's asking us about his da," he finally said. "No one's asking us nothing."

He was her big brother, two years older, thirteen. She could always count on him to know what to do and how to take care of things. It scared Deirdre to see him looking helpless.

She rested her head against the seat and half closed her eyes. The *clickety-clack* of the wheels went on and on and on.

Jimmy was tired and cranky. He kept bumping against her.

"Cut it out," Deirdre told him.

"We go home now!" he demanded.

Deirdre pulled him to her and held him close. "No, not yet." His hair smelled like soap.

I should have gone on singing outside Gallagher's on Friday night, she thought, until my pockets were full of change to bring to Mum.

The train kept on chugging down the track, rolling them away faster and faster, and there was no way even Sean could stop it.

Deirdre sat very still and let herself go numb.

THREE

The cross-eyed boy turned out to be fourteen, a whole year older than Sean and half his size! His name was Aloysius. Because, he told them, he'd been found in a basket on the steps of St. Aloysius Church. What a big, long name for such a runty kid, Deirdre thought.

"You mean you were just left there?" Deirdre said.

Aloysius flared up. "So what? You were left, too."

"I was not!"

"You were, too!"

"Was not!"

"Were, too!"

"Hey, you. Quit bothering my sister," Sean snapped.

That stopped Aloysius's talking for a while.

Deirdre stared out the window. Weeds and some kind of yellow flowers grew alongside the track. There were scraggly bushes and trees and no buildings at all for as far as she could see. When she squinted, it seemed as if the train was standing still and the trees and bushes were speeding by in a blur of all different shades of green. She thought Ireland must look like that. Mum said Ireland was the most beautiful, greenest place you'd ever hope to see—that's why they called it the Emerald Isle.

"There's a Little Bit of Heaven, Sure They Called It Ireland." That was one of their songs. Mum went out singing in the streets after she'd lost the cleaning job, and after a while Deirdre went out with her. She could harmonize just like that, with no one even teaching her how. Mum's sweet voice sang the melody and Deirdre's voice, true and clear as anything, swooped high and low and all around it. It was fun when she went along with Mum, that's when she felt closest to her, but things changed after Jimmy was born. Mum was different, she got that sad, faraway look in her eyes, she didn't talk much anymore, she didn't do much of anything, and then Deirdre started going by herself.

One time a lady listening to her on Rivington Street said, "That voice is a gift from God." It made Deirdre feel so warm and proud. She used to think anybody could sing, just as natural as breathing, but then she found that lots of people couldn't carry a tune at all—Sean, for one. She could hear a song only once and know every note of the melody, even if she didn't get all the words right away. And she didn't have a high little-girl voice like the other girls on the street; hers was deeper and richer. It was truly God's gift to her, she thought; it was the one remarkable thing she had.

The agents handed out sandwiches. It had to be around

lunchtime. Deirdre couldn't tell mealtimes by the grumbling in her stomach because she was hungry most of the time. She tore through the waxed paper—cheese on white bread! And a sugar cookie, too, and half a container of milk. They gave good food on this train!

She didn't realize she was wolfing it all down until she felt Aloysius watching her. She tried to slow up, but it was gone too fast. Jimmy slurped the last of his milk. He licked the sugar crumbs from his lips.

"You want mine?" Aloysius held his food out. "Here."

"You're not gonna eat it?" Deirdre asked.

"I can't eat when I'm excited," he said. "It makes me throw up."

"Hey, thanks!" Deirdre, Sean, and Jimmy split the sandwich. Jimmy got too full to finish all of his, so Deirdre and Sean split his share. They each took a bite of Aloysius's cookie—it was gone in three bites. They had to feed them awful good in the orphanage if he was giving food away, Deirdre thought.

The train made two stops in the middle of nowhere. Each time, Aloysius jumped up and stretched past Sean to look out the window. Nothing was happening, just a couple of people getting on far down the track.

"I guess there won't be a viewing at every single stop," he said, disappointed, when the train started up again.

"They'll tell us when to get out," Sean said.

"Where are we?" Deirdre asked.

"I don't know," Sean said. "Ask the agent."

"I don't want to," Deirdre said. "You think we're out of New York?"

"For sure."

"I need to go," Jimmy said.

The truth was, Deirdre needed to go, too. What was she supposed to do? They'd never stop the train for them, she knew that much.

"What do we do?" she asked Sean.

"Let's go tell the agent," Sean said.

There were four agents sitting in the car among all the kids.

"Come on," Deirdre said to Jimmy. When she got up, her legs felt stiff. She'd been sitting for hours.

They went over to the lady.

"My little brother has to go," Sean said.

"Okay," the lady said.

"But—but—what—?"

"There's a bathroom at the end of the car," the lady said. "Over there."

"A bathroom right on the train!" Deirdre whispered to Sean.

"I knew that," he said.

"Oh, sure."

Sean took Jimmy inside. Deirdre waited her turn. There was an open sliding door and a platform between the train cars with chains on both sides. She went to stand on the platform. It shook with the motion of the train, and she was careful to keep her balance. The ground went speeding by underneath. The air rushing up at her smelled grassy. She peeked into the next car. There were men in suits, men reading newspapers, ladies with hats. Rich people, she thought, going someplace they wanted to go, someplace they knew about.

She wondered if the train might have a dining car. In a movie, she'd seen Clara Bow, the "It" girl, in a dining car: napkins and tablecloths and a waiter carrying a silvery tray. If there even was such a thing in real life. Dining cars, flappers dancing the Charleston on tables, the stock market going higher and higher and people dizzy from getting so rich, debutantes and coeds and movie-star vamps like Pola Negri—on the Lower East Side, all that was as much a fairy tale as "Snow White" and "Little Red Riding Hood."

The bathroom was nice, Deirdre thought. It even had a sink. She washed her hands, but she couldn't find a towel, so she dried them on her skirt. In the cracked mirror hung over the sink, her face looked the same as always, though her life was changing so fast. "I'm Deirdre O'Rourke," she said to herself. The crack went right through the middle of her face.

When she got back to her seat, she found Jimmy sprawled across it. She nudged him around and let him lay his head in her lap. He fell asleep, sucking his thumb noisily. His hair was sandy blond like Mum's, and shafts of sunlight from the window caught bits of it and turned it to gold. He didn't look anything like her and Sean; they had fair skin, too, but they had black hair and black eyelashes. "God put your eyes in with a sooty finger," Mum said. Sean's eyes were blue and hers were brown, but they were cut from the same cloth; that's what Mum said. Mum said Sean could charm the birds out of the trees when he wanted to. Deirdre could almost hear the lilt in Mum's voice. She bit her lip hard so she wouldn't cry.

Jimmy's thumb dropped out of his mouth. She watched his even breathing. There was a tiny sprinkle of freckles across his nose. His eyelids had a line of the palest blue just above where the lashes curved up. Funny, she'd never noticed that before…

All along, there had been a drone of background noise in the car—kids talking, laughing, acting up. Suddenly the sound changed and there was a different kind of buzz. Something was happening. Sean sat up straight, eyes alert and watchful.

The agents were walking through the car. "We'll be there in forty-five minutes. Get yourselves washed up, comb your hair, get your belongings together…"

Throughout the car, kids began combing and straightening and preparing and lining up for the bathroom. Deirdre smoothed the skirt of the brown-and-white dress; it was too long, but it almost fit. The lady agent helped her retie the big bow in the back. Jimmy, jostled awake, whimpered. Sean brushed dust off his new shoes with his hand. Two red spots of excitement burned in Aloysius's cheeks; he was frantically patting his hair down.

The agents were talking, up and down the aisle. "Don't

leave anything on the train." "Be polite: yes, ma'am, and yes, sir." "Best foot forward." "Check under your seats."

Soon, too soon, the train pulled into the station. Aloysius was half out the window. He must have been holding his breath, because when he spoke, he exhaled all of a sudden. "There's nobody there!"

"What, did you expect a brass band?" Sean's voice was harsh.

And then there was a buzz all around. "The courthouse." "They're over by the court." "They're waiting for us at the courthouse."

All the children left the train. Sean carried Jimmy down the steps. There was just a strip of pavement and a little weathered station house. A sign said STRANDSBURG. The S and T were so faded, Deirdre could hardly make them out. A whistle blew, and the train pulled out of the station. She looked back at it; it had begun to feel familiar.

The agents herded them along the street, past one-story buildings and grassy lots and horses tethered to carriages. Some men in overalls in front of the drugstore stared as they went by.

They walked in orderly rows, almost perfect double file, except for the family groups, like Sean and Deirdre and Jimmy, who walked side by side. And there was a huge silence. Not one kid horsing around or carrying on or getting out of line. Deirdre knew Jimmy didn't understand a thing about what was happening, but he caught the silence, too.

FOUR

The train kids lined up on a platform at the front of the large courtroom. Some people sat on rows of benches, relaxed, as if they were there to watch a show. Other people walked back and forth in front of the platform, looking the children over.

Deirdre stood next to Sean, her arms folded tight in front of her chest. Jimmy leaned against Sean's legs; Sean held him close.

All those people, looking them up and down. A boy, around ten years old, said something to his pa and pointed.

Deirdre glanced at Aloysius. His whole body was tilted toward the people; he bobbed up and down with trying so hard. He couldn't stop moving. He swiveled his head, smiling at anybody who came near, a too-big pasted-on smile that creased his cheeks. It made him look like a monkey.

Deirdre stood absolutely still, still as death. Sean kept his face blank; his eyes darted around the room, checking everything.

Men in overalls, men in suits, old ladies, young, everybody studying the train kids as if they were inspecting the fruit at Giambelli's stand.

"What do you think, Mother?" an old man said to his wife. He talked with a funny twang.

"No, doesn't look strong enough to me."

They were far, far away from Rivington Street and Giambelli's.

A lady came up close to Deirdre and peered in her face. "She's a pretty little thing. Too skinny, but—"

"Uh-huh, but look at her—a bad disposition."

Did they think she was deaf, dumb, and blind? She hated them, she hated all of them!

Deirdre, stiff in the still-starchy dress, focused on the floor. Wide wood planks, worn spots under a shiny coat of polish. She curled deep inside herself to shut out their eyes.

"Hello, little lady," a man's voice said.

Deirdre whipped her head up and shot him a furious look.

He backed away.

Some of the kids from the train had been picked out of the lineup. Deirdre watched them follow their new owners down the long aisle.

No one went toward Aloysius.

A young couple drew near. The lady was smiling at Jimmy. "Oh, he's darling. What a beautiful little boy."

She held out her hands. Jimmy put his arms up, and when she lifted him, he wound his legs around her. He rested his head on her shoulder.

We never hugged Jimmy enough, Deirdre thought. No one gave him much attention.

"Look how he's taking to you already," the man said.

"Oh, the little sweetheart," the lady said.

She started to walk away with Jimmy in her arms.

They were taking Jimmy! They were taking Jimmy!

"That's my brother," Sean said hoarsely.

Maybe they didn't hear him, or maybe they pretended not to. They kept going down the aisle between the benches. And Jimmy nestled contentedly against the lady.

"No, wait!" Deirdre cried out. She and Sean scrambled off the platform.

A man agent pulled them back. "You know you have to let him go," he said. He looked at Sean. "It's the best thing for him, you know that." His eyes were kind. "They're good people."

"No! Wait a minute, hold it!" Sean yelled. No one paid attention. The agent kept a firm grip on Sean's shoulders.

Deirdre watched, paralyzed, as the couple carried Jimmy down the long, long aisle. She couldn't breathe. Just before they reached the entrance, Jimmy turned his head and looked back. She could see the confusion on his face. It suddenly hit him that he was leaving them.

"My brudder!" he screamed. "Deedee!"

Inside, Deirdre screamed, too, but only a gasp escaped from her tight throat. Through the doorway and around a corner, and Deirdre couldn't see him anymore. But she could still hear his panicked wail. "Deedee! Sean!"

Deirdre thought, I'll never see Jimmy again.

• • •

They were on a train again. This was a different one, with gray leathery seats. The car wasn't crowded; most of the youngest kids were gone, and some of the middle and older ones, too.

Aloysius sat off in a corner by himself, his head buried in his arms.

"What state was that? That Strandsburg?" Sean asked an agent.

"Pennsylvania."

It was close to evening. It was still hot in the car, though the door at the end was partway open. Miles of fields and an occasional barn rushed by outside.

Deirdre sat cross-legged next to Sean.

"Listen," Sean said. "We know Jimmy's someplace near Strandsburg, Pennsylvania. We'll find him. We'll snatch him back."

She wished she had played more with Jimmy. She wished she'd never been mad and pushed him away when he tugged at her. She wished she'd taken better care of him.

"They took him so fast," Sean mumbled. "I shoulda done something. But it happened so fast."

"It's not your fault," Deirdre said.

A piece of her heart had been broken off forever, she thought. And it was Mum's doing. She would lock Mum out and never, ever miss her or think about her again.

"She's a bad mother," Deirdre said. "She is, and don't say she's not."

"Yeah, but…" Sean said. He sighed. "Okay. Yeah. But maybe she did the best she could."

Sean was always finding a way to defend her. Seemed like there was an invisible thread between Sean and Mum that Deirdre couldn't get hold of.

She remembered that time back on Rivington Street, in the time before Jimmy. They were hungry, bad hungry, and all they had left was a bit of oatmeal. Mum had spooned it out of the pot and onto Deirdre's and Sean's plates.

Deirdre's mouth was watering, but she had shoved her plate back. "You take some, too, Mum."

Sean had kicked her hard under the table. "Eat it."

Deirdre had looked at him, questioning. She'd thought sharing was the right thing to do.

"Eat," he'd whispered fiercely. "You're making her feel worse." Seemed like Sean could always read Mum's heart.

Back then, Mum gave them the last bit of food, and none for herself. But now she'd thrown them to the wind to get blown in all different directions. Even Sean couldn't find any words to make that all right.

Mother cats clawed and fought if you tried to take their kittens. That was true, Deirdre had seen it. She'd blot Mum's face out of her mind's eye.

Through the window, Deirdre saw the sun setting in a blaze of red and orange. It was the most beautiful sunset on the worst of days. Tuesday, August 24, 1927, she thought, the day I lost my little brother.

FIVE

It was night, and Deirdre felt deep-down tired. Was it only this morning that she'd been shaken awake when the agent came for them? It seemed like forever ago since she'd last slept. She felt as if her very soul was worn out. She curled up on the seat with her head resting on Sean's arm. The loud, rhythmic bump of the wheels kept jarring her. But somehow her eyes closed, somehow she dozed…

"Sean!" She awoke in panic—his arm wasn't under her head! She reached out her hand—his seat was empty! "Sean!" Sean was gone, and she couldn't breathe; her chest was filled with the fluttering of a thousand bird wings. "Sean!" she screamed.

"Your sister's hollering for you," someone said.

"What's the matter?" Sean's voice came from far away.

Deirdre peered through the dim light. She made out shapes: seats and sleeping children, and standing near the half-open door, three forms. One of them, leaning against the wall, had Sean's characteristic slouch. The terrible fluttering quieted, and she stumbled toward him.

"What's all the hollering for?" he asked. "You're gonna wake everybody."

"I didn't know where you'd gone to." She clutched his hand.

"We're talking," Sean said.

"...so the littlest and the biggest ones get snapped up," a boy was saying.

Sean nodded.

"This here's Conner and Mike," Sean told her. "They know the score."

"And the leftovers go to the orphan asylum," Conner said.

"Even if they ain't orphans?" Sean asked.

"Listen, once you're on the train, everyone's orphans," Conner said.

"We're not!" Deirdre said.

Conner gave her a look that was part pity and mostly sneer. Deirdre turned toward the tracks rushing by below her. They made her dizzy.

"Are they okay? Those asylums?" Sean asked.

"Some of them feed you good," Mike said.

"They beat you up for any little thing. Little kids wet their beds, they beat them up and make them stand in the cold all night," Conner said. "And if you talk out of turn—"

"Yeah, but they give you three squares a day," Mike added.

"The nuns take it out on the kids, some being bastards

and all, and born in sin. They beat the sin out of you," Conner said.

"Sister Mary Margaret was nice to me," Mike said. "They're nice at St. Francis's."

"So you think it's better to get picked?" Sean asked.

"Hell, yeah," Conner said. "I'm gonna get lucky and get me some rich folks."

An agent came over to them. "Come on, go back to your seats and try to sleep—you have a big day tomorrow."

Sean and Deirdre went through the dark car, back to their places. She heard faint snores. Somebody whimpered. When she sat down, she automatically adjusted her lap for Jimmy's head, and then she caught herself.

"What did they tell you?" Deirdre asked.

"Shhh," someone said.

She moved closer to Sean. "What did they tell you?" she whispered. "The little ones get taken 'cause they're cutest?"

"People want babies to raise up from scratch," Sean said.

"What if Jimmy wets his bed?"

"That pair looked nice," Sean said. "I bet they can't have their own baby. I bet they treat Jimmy like their own flesh and blood."

"You don't know that," Deirdre said.

"No," Sean said, "I don't know that."

The train's long, lonely whistle sliced into the night. The wheels rolling along the track made a racket, echoing through the car.

Sean took a breath. "They acted nice. Jimmy might get a house and toys and everything."

Deirdre couldn't remember their faces that well anymore. The lady had hugged Jimmy. Maybe they would love him. She'd never know for sure. But if they took a baby, they must like babies; there'd be no other reason she could think of.

"What's a bastard?" Deirdre asked.

"When your mum and da never got married."

Deirdre nodded. "That's what I thought. Then we ain't that."

"No."

Jimmy was, though. Jimmy was a bastard. She hoped the couple that took him couldn't tell.

"Why do the people snap up the biggest ones?" Deirdre asked.

"For farmhands. Slave labor, Conner said."

"What about middle-size? Like us?"

Sean shrugged. "Could go either way, I guess."

"I don't want us to get taken," Deirdre said. "I want to go home."

"See, that's the thing," Sean said. "That's why I was asking around."

"What?"

"We're not getting sent home." A muscle twitched in Sean's cheek. "You heard them…leftovers go to the asylum."

"That boy Conner doesn't know everything. I don't like him anyway."

"So listen—we better get picked. Listen to me, Deirdre. Next time, act nice. Smile."

"I won't!" Did Sean expect her to smile and bob up and down like Aloysius? She wouldn't—she was no monkey in the zoo!

"Conner says nobody takes two kids, so we're gonna have to work extra hard to make them want us."

"I don't care, I hate them!" Deirdre said. She wanted to go home, even if it was the street. It was her street.

"Shut up over there," someone muttered.

"Don't be dumb," Sean whispered. "We need to find the best family we can. So when they're looking us over, I'll be picking them, too, you know what I mean? I'll pick out the best ones."

The train barreled through blackness broken up by an occasional light near the track.

"Sean?"

"What?"

"We're going together, right? Not—not like Jimmy."

"The two of us, no matter what," Sean said. "Don't worry. If anybody tries to take us separate, we'll kick up a fuss."

Deirdre let out a breath she didn't know she'd been holding. "Okay."

"We'll Irish-charm them till they're begging for the both of us." Sean gave an abrupt laugh. "Give 'em the O'Rourke blarney."

Deirdre tried to catch the expression on his face, but it

was too dark. Anyway, he didn't sound worried.

"Sean?"

He sighed. "It's the middle of the night. Go to sleep."

He turned himself around like a cat until he found a comfortable way to stretch out. Deirdre sat close to him, touching at every possible point: her feet reached for his leg, her head rested against his shoulder, her hand curled around a corner of his shirt and held it tight.

Seemed like Deirdre had hardly closed her eyes when the agents came through the car shaking everyone awake. They gave out cups of milk, slices of bread, and hard-boiled eggs. Soon daylight came through the windows. And then there was the long line for the bathroom and getting into the extra dress—this one was blue plaid—and putting the now-wrinkled one in the suitcase. Deirdre's eyes felt sandy.

The train slowed down. It passed a station house. It passed a crowd of people waiting on the paved part between tracks.

"Brandon Gap," Sean said.

"What?"

"The sign that went by. Brandon Gap."

The train inched to a screeching stop. Everyone was up and crowding to the doors. Deirdre's hand was rigid around the suitcase handle.

"Stand up straight," Sean said. "Get your head up. Smile when you're getting out." They moved forward.

"Say 'yes, ma'am' and 'yes, sir' when the people talk to

you." Sean was barking instructions at her. "Did you even comb your hair? Get it outta your eyes." He pushed it back with his hand, and she flinched. "Stand straight, will ya?"

Deirdre flared up. "I'm not some prize pig you're taking to market!"

"What?" Sean laughed. "What do you know about prize pigs?"

She'd never seen a pig in her life, Deirdre thought, except in a picture book. That was something Mum would say. There must have been pigs in Connemara…But she was just after wiping Mum out of her mind.

This time, they weren't marched into a town. They lined up along the tracks, and the train stayed, waiting. There was nothing but train tracks and weeds and endless fields as far as she could see.

The people stood still and stared at them. A lot of the men were in overalls. There was a lady with a torn, dirty housedress. One of the agents made a speech and his words—"obligation," "members of the family," "school and church," "properly clothe"—buzzed past Deirdre. Then a few people started walking along the line, getting a closer look, and soon the others followed.

Sean held her hand. "Stay close," he muttered. "Show we're together."

She hung on to his hand. She put her foot on top of his. The sun beat down on her and into her eyes. She squinted. She smelled grass and cinders.

A well-dressed man passed by.

31

"Good morning, sir," Sean said with a smile. The man glanced at him, nodded, and moved on.

A couple stopped in front of them. They looked clean and neat. The lady had crimped brown hair. The man had a mustache.

"Good morning, sir. Good morning, ma'am." Sean had a big, bright smile. How did he get so good at this?

"Well, good morning." The lady smiled back. She was older than Mum and not as pretty. "How are you?"

"Fine, ma'am. Brandon Gap sounds like a fine town."

The mustache man laughed. "It's gosh-darn small. Pass by the general store and the barbershop, and you're out of town."

Sean laughed, too, as if the man had said something funny.

"I understand all of you came from New York City?" the man asked.

"Yes, sir."

"Never been there myself," the man said. "Too big and noisy, with those dark foreigners running around. I hear they're putting up more skyscrapers. I don't see much sense in that."

"No, sir, I don't like those 'scrapers either, much," Sean said.

That was a big fat lie. Deirdre knew Sean was proud of the Woolworth Building, the tallest in the world and right in New York City.

The man and the lady were whispering together.

Deirdre heard "…friendly…good-looking…"

The sun in Deirdre's eyes made her head hurt. The morning's milk tasted sour in her mouth.

Sean put out his hand. "My name's Sean, and this here's my sister, Deirdre."

"He's got a nice, firm handshake, Ann," the man said. "That's a good sign; I can always tell a man by his hand-shake. We're the Hermans."

"Glad to meet you, Mr. and Mrs. Herman, sir and ma'am."

Sean didn't sound the least bit like himself, Deirdre thought. She hated the way he sounded.

But the lady said, "You're a nice, well-mannered boy, Sean."

"Thank you, ma'am." He was even getting his eyes to sparkle at them. How did he do that?

"How old are you?"

"Thirteen, ma'am. I'm in seventh grade and good in my letters and numbers. In history, too—I know all the presidents from Mr. Washington on. Geography's my favorite."

Sean stopped going to school way back, when his shoes wore through. More plain-faced lies! But the lady smiled. Her eyes met the man's.

"Sean. What kind of a name is that?" he asked. "Never heard that one before."

"It's Irish, sir."

"Oh, Irish." The man turned to his wife. A look passed between them.

"Well, that's all right," the lady finally said. "Well, Sean. We have a place down in Culverville—that's ten miles past the state line. Do you think you'd like the country?"

"My sister and me, we love the country." Sean nudged her and Deirdre attempted a smile. "My sister's eleven and real smart for her age, too."

They turned to her for the first time. Deirdre looked down. She felt frozen. She suddenly had to pee.

"And what's your name, little girl?" the man asked.

Sean nudged her again.

"Y-y-yes, s-sir," she stammered. She was stuttering like that crazy John Fallon back home! Her tongue was thick in her mouth.

Sean was talking to them, and they were talking back to him, and she stopped listening to all the show-off lies Sean was telling.

Then everybody quieted down, and the lady said something in the man's ear, and he said, "Go ahead, Ann."

"All right, then." The lady took a breath. "We'd like to take you home with us. We have a nice room for you, Sean, and let's see, a dog, a big friendly sheepdog named Harry, and lots of—"

Sean gripped Deirdre's hand tight. "And for my sister—"

"—and lots of trees to climb, everything a boy would want."

"And my sister," Sean said.

"You see, we're not prepared for two," the lady said.

"Two children is more than we could manage right now."

"She's no trouble," Sean said. "She can take care of herself. You wouldn't have to do a thing. She don't eat much, neither...So take her, too, all right?" He bit his lip. His voice got very low. "Please," he said, so softly Deirdre could hardly hear him.

"No. No, I'm afraid we can't." The lady looked kindly at Deirdre. "She's a pretty little girl, and I'm sure she'll find—"

The man signaled to an agent, and the agent rushed over.

"We'll take Sean here," the man said. The agent looked happy, and the lady smiled, and everyone was smiling at everyone.

"...a few papers to be signed...at the station house... take just a minute..." the agent was saying.

"Papers to be signed" echoed in Deirdre's head. No! They were taking Sean away from her! No! Her body clutched with shock. There was a loud buzzing in her ears.

Sean's voice cut through. "Not without my sister!"

"Now come along," the agent said. He was tugging Sean away from Deirdre.

"I ain't going without my sister!"

The agent pulled at him. Deirdre hung on to his shirt with all her strength. She heard it ripping.

The mustache man took Sean's arm. "All right, let's go. We've got a long ride ahead, and—"

"And it's time to be fixing lunch," the lady continued.

"Do you like fried chicken, Sean?"

"You heard me! I ain't going—"

"Don't worry," the lady said. "You'll get used to us in no time."

"You have to go to the station house now," the agent said sternly as Sean struggled against them. The agent pried Deirdre's hand loose from Sean.

"You can't make me!"

The man dropped Sean's arm. The couple seemed suddenly doubtful. They looked at each other.

"The children get cold feet at the last minute. That's natural," the agent told them. "You know, nervous. Once you get him home with you, he'll be fine."

"I ain't going!" Sean yelled. "Listen, you'll be sorry! I swear to God, I'll wreck your house! I'll burn your damn trees! I'll shoot your damn sheepdog! I'll—"

The couple backed away quickly. Everyone could hear him; all the people were staring at Sean. "Incorrigible" rippled all through the crowd.

After that, no one else came near them.

SIX

They filed back onto the train. The group had thinned out. There were plenty of seats to choose from.

Mike was gone. Conner was still there. And Aloysius.

Sean and Deirdre were just putting their suitcases down when Aloysius rushed over to them, yelling, "You wrecked it!" His face was red and his eyes were teary. "You wrecked it for everybody!"

"What're you spouting off about?" Sean said.

"This lady, she was gonna decide on me, I swear to God she was, she smiled at me, and you had to start hollering about shooting a dog and everybody heard you and you scared her off!"

"I didn't scare nobody off you," Sean said.

"You did! It was your fault! 'Cause you're incorr—incorr—'cause you're no good!"

"You shut up about my brother," Deirdre snapped. She was proud of Sean, proud of the way he could stand up to anybody!

Sean laughed. "It was your cockeyes scared her off, not me."

"She woulda wanted me!" Aloysius clenched his fists. "She woulda wanted me. If not for you, you bigmouth rotten—"

He flailed at Sean, and Sean shoved him hard. An agent was there like a flash. "Break it up, boys!"

"He started it," Sean said. "Tell him to mind his own damn business!"

"He wrecked it for me," Aloysius sputtered. "His fault!"

The agent put his arm around Aloysius's shoulders. "It's all right, take it easy."

Aloysius let himself be led away. They could hear the agent murmur, "There'll be another stop and another chance," and Aloysius's tearful voice, "She wanted me. She did, too!"

The train started up with a lurch. Deirdre and Sean settled down in their seats. They'd picked a new place, nearest the door, where the most fresh air came in; they took window seats opposite each other. The constant rumble of the wheels filled Deirdre's ears.

Aloysius was sitting far from them. His head was bent over his knees. He's still as a statue, Deirdre thought. She would have felt sorry for him, but he'd got Sean in trouble! Trouble was coming their way—the agent was heading straight toward them.

"I didn't do nothing to him," Sean said as the agent

stopped at their seats. "He's lucky I ain't in a punching mood!"

Deirdre expected the agent to yell at Sean, but he didn't. His voice was quiet and sad. "That was a very stupid thing to do," he said.

"What?" Sean said defiantly.

"In Brandon Gap, you—"

"He's dreaming—I didn't keep no one from picking him. Plenty of other kids got taken." Sean narrowed his eyes. "And no one's breaking up me and my sister."

"We'd better talk, Sean. Come with me."

"What for?"

"Come on."

Sean got to his feet reluctantly. He straggled behind the agent. They stood in the vestibule at the end of the car. Deirdre knelt on her seat and leaned over the high back so she could watch them. The agent was trying to say something; he was gesturing with his hands. Sean wasn't giving him chance to get the words out; he kept interrupting. He was standing up straight, with his head tilted forward; he looked fierce and mad. One time, he pointed an angry finger right in the agent's face! But the agent kept on talking and talking, and after a while, Sean was listening and nodding. Deirdre saw his body slump.

It was an awful long talk about not fighting, Deirdre thought. It had to be something else. Sean was standing there looking hangdog. It was something bad.

When Sean came back, the look on his face made her

heart stop. She turned away and looked out the window. She didn't want to hear.

Sean stood in the aisle, awkward. He cleared his throat. "That agent—that Mr. Cole—he's all right."

Deirdre concentrated on the splotches on the window glass. She ran her finger along the dusty metal edge.

"Deirdre. Listen. Mr. Cole says it's a miracle if anybody takes two kids. It don't happen."

Deirdre's head snapped up. "But you won't let them break us up. Will you?"

Sean was silent.

"Will you?" That morning's bread made a hard lump in her stomach, a terrible taste on her tongue.

Sean didn't answer.

"Sean?"

He sank down next to her, his arm grazing hers. When he finally spoke, his voice came out ragged. "Deirdre, we gotta play the cards we're dealt. We gotta play it smart."

"We're staying together!" Deirdre wailed.

"Mr. Cole says I ruined your chances back there, along with mine. He said I was leading the both of us to the orphan asylum."

"I don't care! The orphan asylum would be better."

"No. It's no place for us."

"We'd be together."

"No, that's the thing." Sean was picking and picking at a small rip in his seat's leather. "They keep boys and girls separate. I never thought of that. Mr. Cole says we'd most likely be sent different places. So the best thing to do is find you some good people. Even if it's separate."

"I can't go by myself!"

"Listen to me. You're pretty, anybody would want you, but you got to look friendly," Sean said. "You got to."

"I can't!"

"Here's the plan. I'll check out anybody that talks to you. If they seem okay, I'll give you a go-ahead sign."

That was no kind of plan. He didn't even have a plan.

"You said the two of us, no matter what. You said!"

"I made a mistake," Sean mumbled.

"No! No, that Mr. Cole's the one made a mistake!"

Sean always knew what to do, he could always find an angle.

"Do something! Go tell him—"

"I just told you, he's all right." Sean sounded harsh. "He did us a favor, opening up my eyes."

"How come you're trusting him? He's lying!" Deirdre said.

"No. Ain't nothing in it for him." Sean touched her shoulder. "It's the best way. It's the best we can do."

"I don't care!" She couldn't look at Sean.

They were passing vast expanses of fields. Near the tracks, there were dots of yellow dandelions and puffballs. The heat of the day was gathering, but Deirdre felt cold and clammy, frozen beyond tears.

Sean's voice softened. "I won't go with anyone till after you're picked, I promise," he said. "Okay, Deirdre?"

41

The Italian family on Grand Street ate dandelion greens in salad. Sometimes Deirdre found dandelions growing in cracks in the sidewalk. She liked to blow the puffballs away.

"Deirdre? Okay?"

She shrugged. There no use making Sean feel worse. He was as helpless as she was.

"Listen, maybe we'll both get taken in the same town," he continued. "Maybe we'll live no more than a block away."

The fields sped by in a blur.

"But what if we don't?"

"Maybe we'll get a miracle," Sean said.

Saint Jude was the granter of impossible prayers, Deirdre remembered. She and Sean stopped going to church when their shoes wore out; Mum was ashamed to bring them in barefoot. But I've kept the faith, Saint Jude, Deirdre silently mouthed. Please help me now and keep me and Sean together. Please, Saint Jude. It hurt to lose Jimmy but, God forgive me, not like Sean. Sean's the one I love the most, more than Mum, more than Jimmy, Sean's been there my whole life, I can't lose Sean, please, Saint Jude, I beseech you. Those were the right words, she thought—I beseech you.

She stared at rows upon rows of brown furrows racing past, everything flat, not one hill. She was in the middle of nowhere; she hoped Saint Jude could hear her from here. What would she do without Sean?

"Deirdre," Sean said.

"What?"

"At the next stop…If we can't stay together at the next stop," he said, "I'll find where you are and come for you someday. I swear, on my life. You, and Jimmy, too."

"Don't do that, Sean," she said. "Don't swear on your life." No matter how much Sean wanted to, he might never to able to come for her. Because children had no power, they had to go where they were taken and stay where they were sat, and no one asked them anything. They had no more control over what happened to them than puffballs blown along by the wind.

SEVEN

The name of the place was Greenville. The main street was busy, though it was almost twilight. There were stores and a post office and a hotel with a big porch and horses hitched up to posts. The rolling hills in the distance were the first Deirdre had seen since when—Strandsburg? How long since they'd left the city? Two nights on the train, or three? She couldn't think; her mind was too cloudy. Strandsburg, Brandon Gap…There'd been other stops, too, where they'd been let out to stretch their legs and run around on the platform. But those weren't viewings.

They were lined up at the front of a stage in a theater. The stage was bare except for a piano. Worn maroon velvet curtains hung at the sides. The lights that shone on them caught the glint of spiderwebs. It was too hot. The starch in Deirdre's dress had long ago wilted.

Some of the people came to the edge of the stage and talked to kids, craning their heads up at them. Some of the people walked up the stairs on the side and right onto the stage. There were other people sitting in the rows of seats, lots of them, but Deirdre could see only their silhouettes. There was no movie for them to watch—the train kids were the show.

Nothing seemed real anymore. Deirdre felt removed from her body, as though she were watching herself on the stage, watching her own automatic smile. Sean stood next to her, but there seemed to be vast stretches of space between them. There was a constant rustle of paper as people fanned themselves.

A weathered old woman with bloodshot eyes had talked to her. Sean shook his head no, so then Deirdre stared dumbly at the floor until the woman went away.

Now Sean was giving her a nod. This lady was wearing a clean flowered dress and the man had a pressed shirt. Deirdre forced her lips up into a smile and said, "Yes, ma'am," whenever the lady paused. The lady talked a lot, and that was good—Deirdre didn't have to say much.

"We're Anna and Clem Anderson; we've got that big farm just past Post Road. You might have seen it from the train." She was round, with big round breasts and round pink cheeks. Her hair was blond, wound up in a bun. "Now, let's see, we have four boys at home—Fred's the youngest, he's seven and shy—and our oldest boy Robert, he up and got married but he's living with us for now. And there's Grandpop. A nice regular family."

"Yes, ma'am," Deirdre said.

"Of course, there's chores to be done on a farm. We've

got an acre in corn and four cows. Ever milk a cow?"

"No, ma'am."

The lady laughed. "Didn't think so, you from New York City. Never mind, that's Andy's chore." The pink cheeks quivered when she laughed. "We all pitch in, but I say farm work is a job for the boys. Ain't that right, Clem?"

"That's right," he said.

"Now, you strike me as a good obedient girl, not the lazy kind."

"No, ma'am."

"Our Robert's new wife, God love her, is a sweetheart, but she wouldn't so much as dip a hand in hot water in case it ruined her nails! Ain't that right, Clem?"

"That's right."

Deirdre stared at the pink of the lady's cheeks.

The lady smiled at Deirdre. "Aren't you a pretty one! She's got a face shaped like a heart, now, doesn't she, Clem?" She turned to the man, and he nodded. "It'll be nice to have a pretty little girl in the house."

The lady smiled at Deirdre. She smiled a lot. The pink, round cheeks made her look like a jolly person in a story-book, Deirdre thought. But the smiles never went up to her eyes; maybe they looked empty because they were so very pale blue. There were hardly any lashes around the cold eyes.

"Kind of skinny, aren't you?" she went on. "But you'll fill out in no time on good country cooking...fresh country ham in the oven and biscuits and new-churned butter." She chuckled. "Hope you've got more appetite than you look. But never mind, you'll do fine."

Sean was listening. He was giving Deirdre a definite go-ahead, so she tried chuckling back at the lady, and she was watching herself from some faraway distance.

A man had come onto the stage and went right to Sean. He had a scraggly beard and soiled overalls. His chin was brown with tobacco juice.

"Open your mouth," he said to Sean.

Sean, puzzled, obeyed.

The man suddenly stuck his finger in and felt Sean's teeth. Sean started and snarled, "Do that again and I'll bite it off!"

The man grabbed Sean's arm and felt the muscle. "Healthy and strong enough. You'll do. Come on."

"I ain't going with you," Sean yelled, struggling. "I don't like you!"

"Come along, boy, I can use you." He pulled at Sean.

"Let go!" Sean shouted. He aimed a punch at the man's arm. "I ain't working for you! You smell like shit!" Another punch at the man's chest.

The man let go fast. He went on along the line, muttering, "All the strong ones been taken..."

All around, there were bad whispers about Sean.

"...ornery slum kid...roughneck...did you see what he did?...hooligan..."

It was happening again. No one in Greenville would take Sean now!

The lady went on talking, and Deirdre watched her lips move.

Sean was supposed to be in the same town at least!

"...so if you'd like to come along with us..." the lady said.

Deirdre turned to Sean, pleading. His look at her was hard and fierce. His eyes were telling her she had to do this.

She took a step toward him.

"Go," he muttered under his breath. He half turned and moved away from her.

Deirdre made herself follow the lady and the man. All the way down the aisle, she kept her head turned back. Sean was watching her leave: his eyes were like stone; his body was stiff and his hands were jammed in his pockets.

The lobby was crowded with people coming and going. A table was set up on the side. Mr. Cole, the agent, and three men in suits sat behind it. The people who were taking children waited their turn. Papers rustled, papers were filled out, pens scratched.

Sweat stains blossomed under the arms of the lady's flowered dress. Deirdre followed her to the end of the line. She couldn't feel her legs move. Somehow one foot managed to go in front of the other.

A girl in the navy orphanage pinafore stood in front of Deirdre. Their eyes met and held for a moment. Then each looked away.

"The screening committee," Mrs. Anderson said.

"Reverend Gansworthy, Judge Brown, and Sam Kettles the owner of the hardware store."

"You'd think they could speed this up," Mr. Anderson said. He took out a handkerchief and mopped his brow.

People who hadn't chosen children milled around and watched. A bony woman in a faded gingham dress stared at Deirdre. Some kids who had come with their parents played in the lobby and slid on the stained marble floor. The gold trim on the walls was peeling. A tattered poster— VAUDEVILLE TONITE!—fluttered under the ceiling fan. A movie poster, GLORIA SWANSON STARRING IN…Everything Deirdre saw seemed fuzzy, as if she was looking through gauze curtains.

The gray-haired man in the dark suit was reading out loud for everyone to hear: "Persons taking these children must rear them as members of the family, sending them to school, church, and Sabbath school, and properly clothe them until they are eighteen years old…"

"That's the reverend for you; he can't resist another sermon," Mrs. Anderson muttered.

The scraggly-bearded man, the one who had stuck his finger in Sean's mouth, got in line behind Deirdre. He was pulling Conner along by the wrist. Conner didn't look so tough now; he looked bewildered. A couple came up behind them with one of the big boys. And then a family group with another girl from the orphanage. So children were still being chosen—maybe someone in Greenville would take Sean after all. Deirdre's eyes were riveted to the door from the auditorium. Please, God, she thought, let Sean be next, I'll give anything, anything...

But no one else came, and suddenly time speeded up, she was at the head of the line, the lady signed for her, and it was Conner's turn, and then the last orphanage girl and the agent stood up and shook Conner's hand and patted Deirdre on the shoulder—she couldn't feel his touch, she couldn't feel anything—and he said, "Good luck," and he was leaving and...

The crowd in the lobby parted, and the leftover orphans came through in double file. There was Sean—Sean!—and she could see him looking for her among all the people. He found her, and he marched by half-backward, keeping his eyes on her until the end. Everything inside Deirdre strained toward him, but she didn't move. At the very last minute, just before he went out the big glass doors, he gave a little wave.

The heat was smothering. The room shimmered in front of Deirdre. The man and the flowered-dress lady—Deirdre couldn't remember their names—were talking to her. For all she took in, they could have been speaking a foreign language. "...some errands...the general store...bring the horse and wagon 'round...why don't you wait right here?...back in a jiffy..."

The piercing sound of the train whistle cut through Deirdre's daze. The train was leaving—and with Sean on it! Now she was completely on her own.

EIGHT

Deirdre waited for the Andersons in a corner of the lobby. The three screening-committee men were gathering the papers on the table. Her eyes drifted to the VAUDEVILLE TONITE! poster; it said MAY 4–6. That was long, long ago, when she and Mum, Jimmy, and Sean were together, when she never imagined that it would ever be different...

Deirdre was startled by a tug at her arm. It was the woman in the faded gingham dress who had been staring at her before.

"Come on, quick," the woman said, "before they get back." She took Deirdre by the hand toward the screening committee. Did she mean to steal her away from the Andersons? Deirdre wondered. Not that she'd care; the Andersons made her uncomfortable.

"Excuse me, Reverend Gansworthy?" the woman said.

The tall gray-haired man looked up. "Yes?"

"Well, maybe it ain't my business...um...maybe I shouldn't...but—"

"What is it, Annie?"

"But look at this girl here. She's so young and—it's troubling me and—"

"What's troubling you?" Reverend Gansworthy said kindly. "Come now, out with it."

The other two men on the committee were looking at Annie, too, and she seemed to wilt. Deirdre watched her, puzzled. But then Annie took a deep breath and gathered her courage. "It's the Andersons, sir. You can't let them take her; look at her—just a bit of a girl. It ain't right, that's all. I do the wash sometimes, over at the Andersons when they've got a big load, and I hear things. Don't mean to listen or nothing, I just do my job, but—they ain't fit to take her, and it near breaks my heart to see it."

Deirdre's stomach knotted. She knew she'd seen something creepy in those pale cold eyes. Sean made a mistake; he'd judged too much by the neat clothes and jolly talk. But what did Annie know?

Reverend Gansworthy frowned. "The Andersons are property owners and…"

"And respectable folks," the bald man added.

"Tell us, what kind of things do you hear, Annie?" Reverend Gansworthy asked.

"About why they're taking her, sir, and it ain't like you said, treating her as family and sending her to school and all, 'cause they won't be sending her to any school. It ain't like that."

Deirdre felt a chill creeping up her neck in spite of the

heat in the room. "She's meant for the old man, Mrs. Anderson's pa—he's old, so old he's gone back around to babyhood. Needs his food mashed up and someone to feed him in his bed. And someone to take out his slops and change his nappies and all. And make up a new bed when he messes and wash him up." Annie was holding Deirdre's hand as her words tumbled out; to Deirdre, the warmth of it felt like her only anchor. "That's what they had the daughter-in-law do, no end to it, all day and night—that's why the daughter-in-law run off. He's not right in the head, either, and he'd grab her arm and it was the devil to pry him off. He caught me one time, too. And he has this big stick to thump on the floor when he needs something, and she'd get some good whacks from that stick. So she run off, and the Andersons were saying they'd find a girl off the orphan train to take her place."

Deirdre listened with her heart thundering. She was caught in a trap! She didn't want to take out an old man's slops!

"Are you quite sure about this?" the bald man asked.

"Yes, sir, Judge Brown, sure as anything," Annie answered.

Deirdre looked from one face to another. She needed them to save her.

Reverend Gansworthy said, "I know Annie Albright. I'll take her word," and Deirdre was able to breathe again.

"Why didn't you speak up sooner?" Judge Brown asked Annie.

"I couldn't because... Not in front of the Andersons. I

do the wash for them sometimes, and if the Andersons say I've been listening in, no one's gonna call me for my jobs— but I know right from wrong, and you can't give this sweet little girl to them."

"You did the right thing, Annie." Reverend Gansworthy sighed. "We do our best for these poor unfortunates, and with only a split second to decide…"

"You won't tell them I said anything?" Annie looked around anxiously. "I don't want to be here when they come back."

"Don't worry, we'll keep you out of it," Reverend Gansworthy said. "We'll take care of it."

"Thank you, sir." Annie squeezed Deirdre's hand.

"Thank you," Deirdre whispered to her.

"I hope you get a real good home." Annie hesitated. "Child, I'd take you myself if I could."

And Deirdre wished Annie could, too, as she watched her go.

The last stragglers had left the lobby. Only Deirdre and the three men remained. The whirring of the ceiling fan broke the long silence.

"We made a mistake." Light reflected from Judge Brown's bald head. "Too much of a rush—that's exactly why I hesitated to serve on the committee."

"A natural mistake. Property owners, after all," Reverend Gansworthy said. "We can't do more than trust in folks' goodwill."

The third man, red-haired, turned to Deirdre. "How

old are you, girl?" he asked gently.

"Eleven."

"What's your name?" he asked.

"Deirdre O'Rourke."

The red-haired man gave her an encouraging smile. "That's a pretty name."

"Well, what do you propose we do with her? That orphan train's long gone," Judge Brown said.

The three men stared at her. Deirdre shifted awkwardly.

"Well, someone will have to take her in," the red-haired man said. "At least until we can contact Children's Aid."

"Back there in New York," Judge Brown said. "How long before they can send someone for her?" He sighed. "I suppose we could put her up in the rooming house."

"A child doesn't belong in the rooming house," the red-haired man said. "How would it look? Here we're asking people to open their homes to these orphans, and we ourselves can't manage to—"

Deirdre concentrated on the red-haired man. He was the only one who'd talked directly to her; he was her best hope.

He looked uncomfortable. "I'd take her myself—well, temporarily—if Lydia wasn't expecting…This time it's harder on her than before…"

"I suppose anyone willing to adopt already has," Judge Brown said. "Can't call back the train, can we? A fine kettle of fish!"

"We have to accept responsibility," Reverend Gansworthy said. "Someone has to—"

"It's improper to place a little girl with a widower like me," Judge Brown said. "No woman in the house." He looked pointedly at the minister.

"Yes, I was just about to say—" Reverend Gansworthy drew himself up. "I'll be glad to take her."

He'd hardly looked at her, not once, Deirdre thought. They were deciding about her as if she wasn't there, and she was standing right in front of them as plain as day!

"That's a wonderful thing you're doing, sir!" the red-haired man said.

"Sometimes an opportunity arises to put your faith into action," the minister said. "We should welcome the opportunity to demonstrate simple Christian charity."

"We never expected you to—"

"No, no, that's fine." Reverend Gansworthy cleared his throat. "It's our duty. Mrs. Gansworthy will tend to the girl. If you'll deal with the paperwork—and with the Andersons when they come back…They certainly kept her waiting!"

"Glad to," Judge Brown said. "I'll take care of it."

"Well, child, come along, then," the minister said. "Good evening, gentlemen."

Deirdre hesitated. The red-haired man whispered, "You're in good hands now." A minister was a bit like a priest, Deirdre thought. Anyway, there wasn't a whole lot of choice in front of her, was there? So she scurried to catch up with him.

NINE

Reverend Gansworthy's hair was gray, so he had to be old, Deirdre thought, though he held himself ramrod straight. The tight collar of his shirt seemed about to choke him. He looked so ritzy in his dark suit and all; Deirdre thought he might have a Model T for her to ride in.

She followed him to the big glass doors and was surprised to see that it was dark outside. There was nothing waiting for them on the street—not a carriage, not even a horse and wagon. She tried her best to keep up with Reverend Gansworthy's brisk stride. Past the theater, around the corner, another block...She was relieved that the house turned out to be close by, in town.

Waves of sleepiness washed over Deirdre. She needed to stay alert. She tried to focus. A white picket fence visible in the night. A long dark hallway. Glimpses of brown velvet cushions and lace doilies through a doorway. The woman, Mrs. Gansworthy, wrapping a dark wool robe tight around herself, peered at her.

Reverend Gansworthy explaining, "…the Andersons… Annie Albright told us…nothing to do but…Deirdre O' Rourke…"

And Mrs. Gansworthy's outraged voice, "…springing this on me…no notice whatsoever and no…"

"Now, Margaret, you're married to a minister, remember?"

"I can't forget that for a minute, can I? You expect too much of me!"

"The child's had no supper, Margaret. And she's had a long day."

"The first thing she needs is a good hot bath."

"That can wait. The poor child—"

Mrs. Gansworthy's voice, irritated, "No, it can't wait. Lord only knows what she's carrying!"

"…the right thing…" Reverend Gansworthy, apologetic. "…must set an example…after all, our position…"

"I know, our position." A sigh from his wife. "I suppose we can let her have the upstairs room…"

Mrs. Gansworthy led Deirdre past rooms crowded with stuffed furniture. Then to a bathroom—inside plumbing and a big shiny white bathtub. They had to be rich as Rockefeller, Deirdre thought. The checkered tile floor felt cold to her feet.

"Well, get your things off. Hurry up."

Deirdre sleepily removed her dress. She hesitated when she came to her underpants.

"Stop dawdling. Let's get this over with."

The hot bathwater jarred Deirdre awake. "Hey! It's too hot!"

"It has to be," Mrs. Gansworthy answered. "I don't have any disinfectant."

"I don't have fleas or nothing," Deirdre said.

"Or anything," Mrs. Gansworthy said. "And hay is for horses."

Deirdre looked at her, mystified. What was she talking about anyway?

Mrs. Gansworthy began to scrub Deirdre all over with a cloth. Even at Children's Aid, they'd left her alone to wash herself! But Mrs. Gansworthy's lips were set in a grim, determined line, and Deirdre was afraid to say anything more.

On her head, the scrubbing was much too rough. When her hair was pulled, Deirdre backed away.

"Sorry," Mrs. Gansworthy said. "I want you thoroughly clean before you go anywhere near my mattress."

"Ouch!" Deirdre protested at another tug. Soapsuds streamed down her face.

"Done." Mrs. Gansworthy handed over a towel, and Deirdre dried off her reddened skin. "Look at that bathwater. When was the last time you washed?"

Mrs. Gansworthy held up Deirdre's blue plaid dress from Children's Aid with two fingers, at arm's length. It was soiled and wrinkled. "Is this all you have?"

Oh! The Andersons had taken her suitcase with the brown dress in it!

Mrs. Gansworthy shook her head. "We'll have to get you some clothing right away. First thing in the morning."

Deirdre's heart gave a quick leap. Maybe she was lucky, taken in by rich folks. That's what that boy Conner on the train had hoped for. Mrs. Gansworthy wasn't anywhere near as jolly and friendly as Mrs. Anderson, and look how bad that had turned out! Maybe Mrs. Gansworthy was acting crabby only because she'd been surprised. Maybe she would turn out to be nice, after all.

"Are you hungry?"

Deirdre shook her head. Her stomach had been doing cartwheels all through the long, long day.

"Well, what do I do with you now? You look worn out."

Deirdre nodded.

"I suppose I should put you to bed. Come along."

Mrs. Gansworthy found an old flannel nightgown of her own for Deirdre to put on. The sleeves went way past her hands. Then she handed Deirdre an armful of sheets to carry.

"This way."

She led her upstairs. The hall light shone into a big room. It looked like a storeroom, with suitcases and cardboard cartons lined up along the walls. A bed was in a corner near the window. Its iron frame glimmered in the shadows.

"Very well, then," Mrs. Gansworthy said. "We'll see you in the morning. Breakfast at seven-thirty."

Mrs. Gansworthy closed the door behind her, and the room was plunged into darkness. There was just a bit of moonlight to see by. Too tired to make the bed, Deirdre sank down on the bare mattress. It smelled of mothballs and lavender.

The bed was narrow, but it felt too empty. She was used to Jimmy squeezing in next to her and Sean shoving her legs out of the way. They were always fighting about Sean taking up all the space. How many times had she wished for a bed all her own with lots of room to stretch out? Maybe God was punishing her for wishing for the wrong things. She wanted Sean, Jimmy, someone she belonged with. Where were they now? Tears flowed from her eyes and ran down to her ears. She brushed them away quickly—she mustn't get the Gansworthys' pillow wet!

Deirdre had never been so alone. She couldn't help it, the tears started up again. She clenched her teeth. Well, she told herself, didn't Lucky Lindbergh go all alone in an airplane across the ocean and way over to Europe? And that was flying up in the air with nothing beneath him, and here she was, safe in a warm bed—too hot in flannel—so what was she crying about? Maybe she'd get used to it... But it was dark, with not even the beam of a street lamp. There were strange squeaky noises everywhere.

She sang softly to herself for courage. "April Showers" was just the song to give her comfort, for didn't it tell her that though she might be caught in a shower now, there'd soon be pretty spring flowers blooming in that very spot?

But her voice broke before she ever got to the part about raining violets. It wasn't little April showers that had suddenly changed her life, she thought; it was thunderstorms and hurricanes that had dropped her in this strange place.

She wouldn't cry. She wouldn't!

Everything would be better in the morning, she told herself. She had to look on the bright side. Okay. The lady was going to buy her new clothes, wasn't she? That's what she should be thinking about. Maybe she could have a red dress. Red was her most favorite color. When she, Sean, and Mum got clothes from the Society of St. Vincent de Paul, you couldn't choose colors; you looked for something that kind of fit and wasn't all worn through. The first brand-new clothes she'd ever had were the two dresses from Children's Aid. She felt bad about losing the brown dress.

She curled herself into a tight little ball; she almost wanted to suck her thumb, like Jimmy. Would Jimmy's new people understand about that, or would they get mad? Would they— Before she could finish the thought, she fell into an exhausted sleep.

Deirdre looked around in confusion: morning, sunshine coming through an unfamiliar window. Then yesterday came rushing back, and she swallowed a sob. There was a hungry rumbling in her stomach. The lady—Mrs. Gansworthy—had said breakfast was at seven-thirty. But Deirdre didn't see a clock anywhere in the room. She didn't know what she was supposed to do, until Mrs. Gansworthy called from downstairs, "Deirdre! Breakfast!"

Deirdre picked up her blue plaid dress from the floor and tried her best to brush off the dirt. She couldn't go downstairs in a nightgown, could she? Or should she?

"Deirdre! We're waiting for you!"

She slipped the dress on and followed the sound of Mrs. Gansworthy's voice. Downstairs, there was a whole separate dining room with a round dark wood table where they took their breakfast. At the windows, heavy brown drapes kept the daylight out.

"Well, here you are," Mrs. Gansworthy said. "Did you sleep well?"

"Yes, ma'am."

Reverend Gansworthy smiled at her. "You may call us—let's see—'Uncle Will' and 'Aunt Margaret.' How's that?"

"Yes, sir."

"Uncle Will," he corrected. "Don't worry, you'll get used to us. We hope you'll feel at home."

A cook silently brought a platter of johnnycakes and ham from the kitchen. The food was good, and plenty of it, too.

"...and if the organ needs repair..." Reverend Gansworthy was saying. "...Charlie says...a wheeze..."

Mrs. Gansworthy passed around a basket of biscuits. The cook came in with a coffeepot and cups.

"Milk for the child," Mrs. Gansworthy told her, and then to Deirdre: "You drink milk, don't you?"

"Yes, ma'am, Aunt Margaret."

"Well, that's good. It's good for strong teeth and bones." Then she continued to Reverend Gansworthy, "…so Velma tells me the Travis boy is courting Annabel Brown." She ate daintily, one little nibble at a time. "Might be another wedding before too long."

It was okay that they were talking about things and people she didn't know, Deirdre thought. It felt like a safe place.

"So—you came from New York City, did you?" Reverend Gansworthy asked. "All by yourself?"

"No, with my brothers. Sean and Jimmy. I mean, yes, we came from New York City. From Division Street. "

"You're not from an orphanage?" Mrs. Gansworthy asked. "I thought they were all orphans."

"We're not," Deirdre said.

"What about your parents, then?" Mrs. Gansworthy asked.

"There's just our mum."

"I see." Mrs. Gansworthy frowned, studying her, and Deirdre felt herself shrink. "Your mother sent you off on that train with the two sons? Why did—"

"Now, Margaret," Reverend Gansworthy interrupted. "Deirdre, I think you'll find Greenville pleasant and friendly. We have just about everything. The new school was finished just last year, there's a fine old hotel, we even have a theater with vaudeville shows coming through twice a year. The Victoria—that's where you were yesterday. A small town by city standards, I suppose, but I think you'll like living in Greenville."

"It sounds nice," Deirdre said. She was grateful to him for changing the subject. Then Reverend Gansworthy read the paper awhile before he left for church. Mrs. Gansworthy had a second cup of coffee and stared off into space.

Deirdre looked around the room. Those drapes had to be velvet, real velvet! There was a painting on the wall in a shiny gold frame; the picture was dark, with black horses and a cloudy sky. There were pretty china doodads on the sideboard and a cute kitten cream pitcher on the table. Deirdre picked it up to get a better look.

"No!" Mrs. Gansworthy's exclamation made her jump. "Put it down. Careful!"

"Sorry," Deirdre mumbled. She put it down extra-gently. "I won't break anything, I promise."

"That's Staffordshire. Don't ever touch it." Mrs. Gansworthy looked at her with a worried frown.

Deirdre wondered why Mrs. Gansworthy seemed so mad at her—she hadn't done anything! But then Mrs. Gansworthy sighed and said, "All right, no harm done. Let's go and get you that clothing now. You'll need school dresses and a coat and…"

So Deirdre walked down the street with Mrs. Gansworthy with almost a skip—going shopping!—and thought that maybe Mrs. Gansworthy did like her, if she was buying her dresses and all. School dresses and a coat! That was the berries!

They stopped off at the church. They went in the side way, where Reverend Gansworthy's study was. Deirdre tried not to be impatient. She guessed Mrs. Gansworthy had to see him for something, something she'd forgotten to tell him at breakfast, and then they'd go on to the store in a minute…But Mrs. Gansworthy only waved at him as they passed his study door.

She took Deirdre into another room. There was a bin— a used-clothing bin!

Deirdre looked up at Mrs. Gansworthy, only looked at her, without a word. But Mrs. Gansworthy must have read Deirdre's mind, because her lips pinched in an angry line. Deirdre could guess exactly what Mrs. Gansworthy was thinking, too: Beggars can't be choosers.

"Don't turn your nose up," was what Mrs. Gansworthy actually said. "These are perfectly clean, serviceable clothes, donated by members of our congregation for…" And she went on. "There's no place for vanity in a pure Christian heart…"

Deirdre saw the stitching from hems that had been let out once too often, the patches of worn shininess. It was all familiar. Nothing had changed, except that now she was alone, without Sean or Jimmy or Mum.

For the rest of that week, Deirdre wondered: What did the Gansworthys want with her?

They weren't looking for a daughter in her, that was for sure. They mostly ignored her, and sometimes it seemed as if they barely remembered her name. Reverend Gansworthy spent most of his time in his study or visiting members of "his flock" all over the county; he did have a car, after all, and that's what he used it for. Mrs. Gansworthy never yelled at her, except for that one time about the Staffordshire kitten, whatever Staffordshire was, so she wasn't exactly mean, but well, at least the Gansworthys didn't take her in to be a servant, either. There was the cook, and a cleaning girl came in twice a week. Mrs. Gansworthy gave Deirdre a little chore, because "idle hands are the devil's workshop." But it was easy: Deirdre helped the cook shell peas. And then she had nothing to do. She spent lost, lonely hours in the musty gloom of the living room, breathing in the faint smell of mildew and listening to the radio serials.

The Gansworthys had the cleaning girl take the suitcases and cardboard cartons out of Deirdre's room and up to the attic. They brought down an old dresser with drawers, just for her. They'd told Deirdre to call them "Aunt Margaret" and "Uncle Will"—though she couldn't bring herself to do it. So it seemed like they intended to keep her, at least for a while. But why?

TEN

On Sunday morning, the reverend left early for church. Later, Deirdre walked down the street with Mrs. Gansworthy. Mrs. Gansworthy wore a silky navy dress. The white flowers on her navy straw hat trembled with every step she took.

"Can I go in without a hat?" Deirdre asked.

"Yes, I told you, didn't I?" Mrs. Gansworthy said. "It's perfectly all right."

Deirdre felt funny about that. She'd never go into church at home without at least a hanky on her head.

"It's really okay?" she asked nervously.

"I said yes." Mrs. Gansworthy blew out an exasperated breath. "I know they meant to place Catholic orphans with Catholics, it's better that way, but there're hardly any in Greeenville. So just do as I do during the service."

"A lot of the orphans are in Greenville, aren't they?" Deirdre hadn't seen anyone from the line in the theater lobby yet; she was longing for a familiar face.

"Maybe one or two. I heard people came to the viewing from counties for miles around. Stop asking so many questions. You're giving me a headache."

Mrs. Gansworthy had said Sunday School would start next week, after regular school did. But Deirdre hoped that maybe she'd get to meet some kids today. She didn't know a single person in Greenville to talk to or play with. She decided to risk just one more question.

"Will there be lots of kids in church today?" Deirdre asked.

Mrs. Gansworthy raised her eyebrows. "The normal amount of children, I suppose. We don't have families of ten the way they do in the slums. And 'kids' are baby goats."

What about baby goats and slums? Sometimes Deirdre couldn't make head or tail out of what Mrs. Gansworthy was talking about.

At least she'd get to see some kids today, Deirdre thought. And they'd see her. She thought she looked nice. She was wearing her best dress. It was like a party dress, with little blue and pink flowers and puffed sleeves. She tied the wide blue belt extra-tight so the dress didn't hang too big on her. It hardly seemed used, except for a yellowish stain on the skirt, and that was well hidden by the deep folds and the flowers. After the cleaning girl had washed and ironed it, it looked fresh and pretty. Just imagine, she thought, someone doing my laundry! Maybe I struck it lucky after all.

At the church steps, there was a flurry of "Good morning,

Mrs. Gansworthy" and "Good morning, Margaret." Deirdre could see the extra respect in the greetings. That proved she was with good people, didn't it?

"Good morning, Margaret. Now is this the little orphan girl we've heard so much about? Isn't she sweet!"

"Yes, this is Deirdre O'Rourke," Mrs. Gansworthy said.

"Deirdre? What an unusual name." The lady smiled at her. "Where are you from, dear?"

"New York City," Mrs. Gansworthy said, before Deirdre could answer for herself. "It's such an adjustment, but she's coming along quite nicely, bit by bit."

What was "coming along"? Deirdre wondered. She didn't think anyone in Greenville knew anything about her. What had that lady heard?

When they entered the church, Deirdre was surprised by the brightness. Sunlight came through the clear glass of the high arched windows and washed over the light wood of the pews and the plain white walls. There were no statues. There was no holy water anywhere she could see. It was nothing like beautiful old St. Malachy's on Chatham Square, with stained-glass windows glowing red and blue in the dim light, and the Stations of the Cross, and the faint scent of smoke and incense... But up front, behind the altar, there was a big wooden cross. It's nice here, Deirdre thought, and I can still be Catholic in my heart.

Deirdre looked around as they went up the aisle. The pews were filled—grownups, family groups. Old people. Squirming little kids. All those people, and not one person she knew.

Deirdre saw three girls leaning toward one another; they looked as if they might be her age. One was pretty, with fat blond braids. They watched Deirdre going up the aisle behind Mrs. Gansworthy. As she passed, Deirdre gave them a hopeful smile. They stared at her. And then, behind her, she heard whispering. She glanced back: the blond girl was pointing at her, and they all were laughing! Deirdre turned away quickly. She bit her lip. What was wrong?

Mrs. Gansworthy smoothed down her dress as she and Deirdre slid into a middle pew. The service started with organ music, and then the people were singing. Deirdre didn't know any of the songs, but the music was peaceful and soothing. Maybe those girls hadn't been pointing at her at all. Maybe she'd imagined it because she still felt so strange in Greenville. *I won't feel this strange forever,* she told herself.

The last notes of one hymn trailed off and the organist played the opening chords of another. "Amazing Grace"! Surely it was a sign from heaven to lift Deirdre's spirit, even more than the rays of sunlight reaching to her through the window. She'd sung that true, simple melody a million times, in front of Gallagher's, in front of Slapsy Maxie's—a song that made the toughest men reach deep into their pockets, a song that warmed her on cold sidewalks, on rainy nights.

So now Deirdre sang out with the rest of the congregation. The simplicity of the melody invited embellishment, and she harmonized, her voice ringing out.

And wasn't this song a gift from God, here to give her

courage in this far-off place? "Amazing grace," she sang, clear and joyful, "how sweet the sound…"

Some people in front turned to smile at her. "I once was lost…" She smiled back, full of heartfelt emotion. "…but now am found…"

It didn't register right away that the jab in her side came from Mrs. Gansworthy's elbow. Deirdre turned to her, startled. "…was blind, but now I see…"

"Stop that," Mrs. Gansworthy hissed.

Deirdre's song ended as abruptly as a faucet being turned off. "But—I—" What had she done now, she wondered.

"Stop that showing off." Deep lines formed between Mrs. Gansworthy's eyebrows. "Pride is a sin."

But her voice was the best thing about her! She *was* proud of it. Could that be a sin?

Mrs. Gansworthy nudged her again. "You can sing," she whispered, "but quietly, along with everyone else."

Deirdre blindly shook her head. That seemed to make Mrs. Gansworthy angry again, so Deirdre mumbled, "I don't know the words."

Mrs. Gansworthy gave her a hard look.

Deirdre blinked back the tears that suddenly threatened to come up. Mrs. Gansworthy didn't like anything about her, that was easy enough to see.

When Reverend Gansworthy started his sermon, Deirdre couldn't listen. She stared dully at the wooden back of the pew in front of her, and his words drifted by her.

"…flappers, sheiks, and ungodly flaming youth… immigrants and anarchists in our cities…yes, we must hate the sin, but raise up the sinner…"

A fly buzzed, and Deirdre's eyes followed it as it zigzagged toward the window.

"We must temper righteous anger with compassion. We must show compassion for the wretched refuse of the cities, for the lowest among us…"

Deirdre squirmed on the hard wooden seat and glanced at Mrs. Gansworthy. A small, satisfied smile flitted over her lips. She didn't look angry anymore.

"…each and every one of us, in his own way. Yes, when the opportunity for an act of simple Christian charity arises, we must gladly rise up to meet it…"

A fly buzzed back along the aisle. Deirdre wondered if it was the same one. It should have managed to get out by now; the side windows were open wide to let in the breeze.

Reverend Gansworthy's voice hit a peak. "Didn't we witness a train of misery and neglect, as sad a train as ever rode these rails? Mrs. Gansworthy and I were glad to serve, to take in a wretched orphan child."

The last words brought Deirdre to sudden, rigid attention. She gasped. He was talking about her! Her eyes darted in all directions in a panic. People were turning around and staring at her. She didn't know where to look. Heat rose in her face.

There was no place to hide in this bright, sunny room. She tried to focus on the floor at her feet, but the floorboards wavered in front of her eyes. Reverend Gansworthy's speech went on, but "wretched orphan child" played over and over in Deirdre's mind. She wanted to curl up tight and become small and invisible.

Now Deirdre understood. She was there to show the whole town how good the Gansworthys were. She was nothing at all.

ELEVEN

Deirdre started school the next week. Everything in the building looked much brighter and cleaner than in her city school; it made her feel hopeful. And she was so glad to have someplace to go, someplace away from the Gansworthys.

She was assigned to the sixth grade. Miss Harrow, the teacher, had Deirdre stand in front of the room. "Class, this is Deirdre O'Rourke," she said.

Deirdre smiled, though her lips quivered a little. A freckled girl in the front row smiled back. Maybe we'll be friends, Deirdre thought. Maybe being the new kid won't be that hard.

But then she saw that girl from church, the one with the fat blond braids, sitting in the third row.

Miss Harrow went on. "Deirdre came on the orphan train from far, far away." Her voice turned syrupy. "So I want everyone to be extra considerate and helpful and make her feel right at home. Can you do that, class?"

"Yes, Miss Harrow," the class sang out together.

There were some snickers.

Deirdre lowered her eyes to the floor. She'd thought she could slip in with the others like a regular kid. Miss Harrow's introduction was almost as awful as Mr. Gansworthy's sermon in church last week.

All through the morning, all through the fractions that she didn't understand and the vocabulary words that she didn't know, Deirdre felt the whispers and pitying looks and curious stares.

At midmorning recess, some kids surrounded her and shot questions at her.

"Did you live in an orphanage? Did they feed you?"

"How did your parents die?"

"Cut it out, Joey! Can't you see you're making her feel bad?"

"I'm just asking."

"Well, don't, 'cause Miss Harrow said to be extra considerate!"

"When you're on the train, do they give you away to anybody that wants you?"

"Where are your grandparents and aunts and uncles and stuff? How come they didn't keep you?"

"'Little Orphan Annie is my favorite comic."

"Don't worry." The freckled girl took Deirdre's hand. "I'm Gwendolyn. Me and Dorothy, we'll help you. You'll be our project, okay?"

Deirdre turned to her, startled. "Your what?"

"We'll kind of adopt you and teach you manners and stuff and take care of you."

Deirdre tore her hand away. "I'm no orphan!"

"Miss Harrow said."

"She doesn't know." Deirdre bit her lips. She didn't want their pity! "I've got a mum and brothers, and they're coming for me any day." She smoothed her dress, the one with the little blue and pink flowers that she'd worn to church. She looked as nice as any of them! "My mum was sick for a while, but she struck it rich and she sends me stuff, party dresses like this and stuff, and she's coming for me soon as she can."

"How come you talk so funny? Where are you from anyway?"

"New York City. And you're the ones talk funny!" It was true, Deirdre thought. In Greenville, they had a real peculiar way of pronouncing words.

"Noo Yawk!" Some of them laughed. "Noo Yawk!"

"Mum! What's that?"

"You're the ones need to learn manners," Deirdre said.

"Oh yeah?" Norma, the girl with the fat blond braids, stuck her face into Deirdre's. "You're a liar!"

"Am not!"

"If you struck it so rich," Norma continued, "how come you're wearing my old dress?" She turned to the circle around them and laughed. "Remember my birthday party when my little brother threw up? The stain's still on the skirt, so I gave it to charity."

Deirdre's face burned. That was why Norma had pointed and laughed at her in church. That was why!

"Vomit girl! Vomit girl!" Norma pranced around her, her beautiful blond braids bouncing in the sunlight.

All Deirdre could see was the smirk on that rosy-cheeked face, and her fist shot out.

"Fight! Fight!" the cry went up.

Norma didn't even know how to make a fist, Deirdre thought; all she could do was open-handed slaps and hair-pulling. Deirdre got her good, on the nose and on the chin, before the recess teacher pulled them apart.

Well, she'd stood up for herself, Deirdre thought, and she sure got the best of Norma—she wished she could tell Sean about it! Now they'd have to respect her.

But it didn't work that way. In Greenville, girls didn't fight. Certainly not punching, like boys. They stared at her, shocked.

Maybe it would have blown over if Miss Harrow had punished her and made her stay after school like anybody else. But Miss Harrow just shook her head and looked sorry. She told Deirdre that her adjustment might take a long time, but they'd be patient and understanding. Miss Harrow said it wasn't Deirdre's fault that she came from a bad environment. She was reading about a new science called psychology, and she'd work with Deirdre and help her improve and the other children would be a good influence.

Deirdre didn't understand all of Miss Harrow's words

about environment and that new science, but it was clear she thought there was something deep-down wrong with Deirdre. And the class followed her lead.

No one ever wanted to play with Deirdre at recess. She'd stand by herself and watch the others laugh and run. Then one day, among a crowd of eighth graders jumping rope, Deirdre saw an orphan train girl; it was the one who'd been in front of her in the screening-committee line! At first, Deirdre wasn't sure it was the same girl. She'd had stick-straight dishwater-colored hair, and now it was all shiny corkscrew curls. She wore a pink jumper with embroidery and a full, full skirt; she looked like a rich kid. Deirdre looked more closely—it was her! It was almost like seeing someone from home! She thought the girl's name was Peg—yes, it was; she remembered thinking of the song "Peg o' My Heart" when she'd first heard her name on the train.

Deirdre dashed over, excited. "Peg!"

The girl whirled around, her eyes wide and startled. "Elise," she hissed. "My name's Elise now."

"I'm Deirdre. Remember me from the train? Remember my brother Sean? And Jimmy?" It felt so good to find someone who knew something about her! She had a million things to say! "Remember when—"

"I don't remember any of that!" the girl interrupted.

"My brother Sean, remember? The one with the blue eyes; he was always getting in trouble with the agents and—"

"I don't know anything about that." The girl looked

angry. "I have a family, they named me Elise, and I don't remember anything from before. Not a thing!" She turned away from Deirdre.

Deirdre backed away awkwardly, as stunned as if she'd been slapped.

For a moment, she'd thought she could have a friend. For a moment, she'd thought she could talk about Sean and Jimmy to someone who'd actually seen them, someone who knew they existed somewhere in the world. She wouldn't bother Peg again. She sort of understood. Peg wanted to be like everyone else, not "the poor orphan girl." That's what I want, too, Deirdre thought, but the Gansworthys and Miss Harrow won't let anyone forget for a minute that I'm here on charity.

Deirdre stayed alone at recess, as lonely as a cloud. The days and weeks wore on. No matter what she did, she couldn't make it better.

She wore her blue plaid dress dress from Children's Aid almost every day so she wouldn't be caught in somebody else's old clothes again; they noticed and whispered about that. Norma said she smelled. But that wasn't true. It wasn't!

On September 30, Babe Ruth hit his sixtieth homer! Everyone in the class was talking about it. Deirdre knew Sean would be talking about the Babe, too, at that very moment, wherever he was. She could almost hear the excitement in Sean's voice. Wherever he was, and nowhere nearby—it was like a knife slicing through her. That's when

Charlie Davis stuck his face into hers and chanted, teasing, "Noo Yawk Yankees, Noo Yawk Yankees," and Deirdre, tears welling up in her eyes, pounded and pounded at his grin; he got a nosebleed. Miss Harrow was upset. "I won't allow violence here!" she said as she mopped up the mess. "I'm losing patience with you, Deirdre O'Rourke."

In October, the bitter smell of burning leaves hung in the air. Dried sunflower heads bent down to the ground. Frances handed out Halloween party invitations to every girl in the class except her. Deirdre didn't make a sound or move a muscle. She hoped no one would notice. But Frances came over to her, with that self-important look on her face. "I'd invite you," Frances said out loud in front of everyone, "but my mother said I can't. She says you're a bad influence and a papist, too."

Whatever that meant! Deirdre couldn't stop herself—she kicked Frances hard in the shin and watched Frances's snobby expression change to whimpers. Frances ran and told Miss Harrow. "I give up!" Miss Harrow exploded. She said Deirdre would just have to stay away from everyone, at recess and in class, too, until she "overcame her savagery from the slums."

Deirdre didn't have anyone to play with in school.

She didn't have anyone to play with after school, either.

Maybe the teacher was right; maybe there was something deep-down wrong with her. She had to keep reminding herself that she used to have friends. Most people back in the neighborhood had liked her. And Sean. Sean loved her. Sean said he'd find where she was and come for her. He'd sworn on his life!

Until then, the best way to keep out of trouble, Deirdre thought, was to be very quiet and fade into the background. She felt shriveled up inside, as dry as the autumn leaves that swirled in the relentless Kansas wind. If Sean didn't come to rescue her soon, she'd crumble, just like the leaves crunching under her feet.

TWELVE

Abigail, the Gansworthys' cleaning girl, told Deirdre, "You should be outside playing instead of moping around inside the way you do."

Abigail was young, but she had an old woman's sour expression. She had a long, narrow nose and close-together squinchy eyes.

"The other place I work, the girl plays outside with her little friends every afternoon after school," Abigail continued.

Deirdre wished she would shut up. She could guess why Abigail was bothering her: the Gansworthys weren't home and Abigail wanted to get rid of Deirdre, too, so she could sit down and rest for a while without anyone seeing her.

Deirdre sat in the gloom of the living room and leafed through old magazines. She wished she had someplace to go.

She tossed an issue of *The Saturday Evening Post* aside and went to the living-room window. It faced the backyard, and she could see the collie in the Crowells' adjoining yard. Every time she'd looked out, the dog had been there, chained to a post near the back door. The dog went as far as his chain would allow. He'd worn away the grass and left a brown track along his path.

The collie came to the end of his chain and stopped, his long nose pointed into the distance. Deirdre could hear him whine deep in his throat; it was the loneliest sound, she thought. She wasn't used to dogs—and this one was big!—but he didn't seem that fierce...

Deirdre went into the yard and leaned over the fence. The dog spotted her. He barked and Deirdre, startled, took a step back. But his tail was wagging; she thought that meant he was friendly.

Deirdre climbed over the fence for a closer look, but she was careful to keep out of his reach. She was scared. Back home skinny stray dogs ran through the streets in wild packs; they'd growl and bare their teeth. Dogs could be dangerous.

But this dog wasn't growling. He strained at the chain with his tail wagging a mile a minute. He didn't look mean. He only seemed excited.

Deirdre took a cautious step toward the dog. His hair was long and light brown, with lots of white at his chest. The ruff of fur around his neck looked so soft, she almost wanted to touch it...

The dog cocked his head and looked hopefully at Deirdre. Now he was making high little yips. He seemed hungry for company, Deirdre thought; she sure knew what that felt like.

"Who's out there?" Suddenly Mrs. Crowell was in the doorway, and Deirdre sprang back. Was she going to get in trouble again?

"It's only me—I'm—I'm not doing anything," Deirdre stammered. "I only wanted to see the dog, I—"

"That's okay." Mrs. Crowell smiled. "Poor guy, I guess he's lonely."

"Oh. Um—does he bite?"

"Rex? Heavens, no! Rex wouldn't hurt a flea."

"Can I—is it all right if I pet him?"

"Sure. Just don't let him off his chain." Mrs. Crowell turned to go inside. Over her shoulder, she said, "Our boy Robbie's off at college, so there's no one paying much attention to the dog now…"

Deirdre hesitated—he was so big. But his dark brown eyes were pleading with her. She took a breath and went over to him. He jumped at her, his front paws on her chest. She was a little scared, but she touched the soft ruff at his neck. Her fingers ran through the long fur, and she felt the warmth of his body. She could feel him quivering under her touch.

When she went to sit on the back steps, he followed. He sat at her side, pressing against her as close as he could get. His doggy smell was nice—like grass and leaves. Deirdre was proud of herself for not being afraid of big dogs anymore; she wished Sean could see.

"I bet you've been missing your boy," she said. "Don't worry, he'll come back to you." She felt foolish talking to a dog, but his eyes watched her mouth as if every word she said was important. He'd taken to her right away, she thought. He liked her.

And then Rex surprised her—he licked her cheek! His tongue was wet and sandpaper rough. Deirdre laughed as she wiped her cheek. She felt as if she'd been kissed.

Now Deirdre had something to do after school. She'd go straight to the Crowells' yard and Rex. He'd be there waiting for her. He was too dignified to run around in circles like a silly puppy, but he was obviously happy to see her. Sometimes they played. If she threw a stick straight up in the air, he could jump and catch it in spite of his chain. Sometimes they rolled on the ground. Sometimes she just sat next to him on the Crowells' back steps and kept her arms around him. She buried her face in the furry ruff around his neck. She wished Rex could hug her back. She knew he would have if he could.

With Rex, Deirdre felt like her real self. At school and with the Gansworthys, she kept very quiet. Making herself invisible was the only way she knew to avoid making more mistakes. She kept her voice buried deep down inside.

On November 8, Deirdre's twelfth birthday came and went, and nobody knew. She wondered if Mum or Sean was thinking of her. Back home, they didn't have enough money for birthday presents. In Greenville, other kids had parties; in school the next day, they'd talk about the cake and the presents and the games. Even if the Gansworthys had wanted to give her a party, she had no one to invite.

"You'd come, wouldn't you, Rex?" She scratched behind his ears and laughed. "You'd wear a funny hat and sit at the Gansworthys' table and eat off the *Staffordshire!*"

She didn't think the Gansworthys noticed that she had no "little friends." That was okay; at least they didn't nag her like Abigail did and make her feel ashamed. They didn't notice her at all unless she was in the way. She tried to think of good things about the Gansworthys. She got all the food she wanted, didn't she? They didn't make her work hard or beat her or anything. Now that it was getting cold with the end of autumn, they gave her an extra woolly blanket. And they'd saved her from the Andersons.

"I try to be grateful," Deirdre told Rex, "but I'm not. Maybe I'm really bad."

The dog's devoted eyes told her that she wasn't.

"I hate it here," Deirdre whispered as she smoothed down the long silky fur. "Except for you."

She missed the city with its busy streets; there was always something happening and something to look at. There was never anything different in Greenville—except for one special day in the middle of November.

It was a Saturday afternoon, and Deirdre was going to the bakery with Mrs. Gansworthy when they saw a big commotion on Main Street. In spite of the drizzle, a whole lot of people, both kids and grownups, were standing around and talking excitedly. Mrs. Randall was in the center of the crowd. Gwendolyn from her class was there, too.

"What's going on here?" Mrs. Gansworthy asked.

"You'll never believe it!" Gwendolyn's cheeks were bright red from the cold. "There's a talking picture at the Victoria! The Randalls just came from there. *The Jazz Singer!* Al Jolson talks and sings from the screen!"

"Hmmph," Mrs. Gansworthy said. "We read something about that in the newspaper. It has to be a phonograph record. Some kind of trick."

"No, ma'am, Mrs. Randall saw the actors talk and sing themselves! It's magic!" Gwendolyn's eyes were big and round. "We're all going to the three o'clock show!"

"Honestly, Margaret," Mrs. Randall said, "it's amazing!"

Deirdre longed with all her heart to see that magic talking movie. Al Jolson singing from the screen! Could she ask?

Mrs. Gansworthy looked down at her. "I suppose you want to go, too?"

"Oh, yes," Deirdre breathed. "Can I?" Sometimes Mrs. Gansworthy was nice to her; it was confusing.

"May I," Mrs. Gansworthy said. "Yes, you may."

Deirdre flushed. She wished Mrs. Gansworthy wouldn't correct her in front of everyone.

Mrs. Gansworthy handed her a quarter. "Thank you, Aunt Margaret," she prompted.

Deirdre was just about to say "thanks" on her own and Mrs. Gansworthy didn't give her the chance! "Thank you, Aunt Margaret," she parroted.

"All right, then, go along with Gwendolyn and the girls."

Gwendolyn couldn't refuse in front of Mrs. Gansworthy. "We better run and get seats," she said. "Everyone in town's going."

"Some people will believe anything," Mrs. Gansworthy muttered.

Deirdre slip-slid on the wet street to the Victoria along with Gwendolyn and a bunch of girls from her class. There was enough excitement to carry her along with the others; for once, she felt part of things in Greenville. The theater was filled with people. The steampipes hissed and there was the smell of wet wool.

It was Deirdre's first time back inside the Victoria and she was filled with sudden dread. She remembered how numbly she had walked down this same aisle. The movie screen hid the stage where she had stood on display, but Deirdre knew it was there and she remembered...

Music came up along with the opening credits. It might be a phonograph cranked up behind the screen, Deirdre thought with dismay. Mrs. Gansworthy might be right.

But then all other thoughts dissolved because she was seeing a miracle! When the actors moved their mouths, she heard their voices and words! And the songs! They were talking and singing themselves, just as if they were right there! Al Jolson played a cantor's son from the Lower East Side of New York City. The street scenes in the movie looked familiar, almost like Rivington with the pushcarts and all, though she couldn't spot anyplace she knew. It looked enough like her old neighborhood to make her breath catch… No, there was no one left there for her anymore. Not Sean. Not Jimmy. And no use in thinking about Mum at all.

Al Jolson's singing, rich and full, came pouring out of his mouth! How could that be? Deirdre stared at the screen in amazement. Al Jolson wanted to be a jazz singer, though his father wanted him to be a religious singer in the synagogue, but he went on stage anyway. It was wonderful!

The other kids were as transfixed as she was. Afterward they stood outside in a big group, and everyone asked her questions.

"Is that where you're from?"

"Did you live in a tenement?"

"Do you know Al Jolson?"

They crowded around her. She answered as best she could, though she didn't know what "tenement" meant. Afterward, they all walked down the street together, and she was with them instead of on the edge by herself. The girls started singing "Swanee," and Deirdre joined in. She sang very softly so no one could say she was a show-off or prideful. She longed to sing full out—some of Jolson's songs were her old songs! But she felt a warm glow inside, in spite of the fierce wind whipping her hair.

When Deirdre turned the corner to the Gansworthys' house, Gwendolyn even said, "See you Monday."

Deirdre let herself feel hopeful about school on Monday.

But when she went to jump rope with the others at recess, Norma said, "No, you can't play with us." The afternoon of *The Jazz Singer* was only a fluke, a bit of Al Jolson's stardust rubbing off. Deirdre felt even worse because she'd had that one sweet moment of belonging.

I don't fit in here and I never will, Deirdre thought. But she was afraid to run away all by herself. Sean was tougher and smarter; he'd figure out where to run. But why didn't he come for her? He knew she'd been left in Greenville. He could have found her, easy. Mum was willing to give her away and Jimmy was too little to remember her for long, but Sean... He couldn't have forgotten about her—could he?

THIRTEEN

The days grew shorter, an icy wind cut through the town, and Thanksgiving came. The Gansworthys had a big feast. Mrs. Gansworthy had fussed with the cook for days, and Abigail worked extra time, too. Some of the people from church were invited, and Reverend Gansworthy's niece and her husband and their twin five-year-old girls. There was turkey—Deirdre had never eaten real turkey before—and stuffing and all kinds of vegetables and sweet potatoes and two kinds of pie, apple and cherry!

They put Deirdre at the end of the table with the two five-year-olds, but that was okay because Deirdre wasn't going to talk to anyone, anyhow. Mrs. Gansworthy had been nervous about the big dinner, and she'd spoken to Deirdre about manners ahead of time: "Children are meant to be seen, not heard" and "Don't speak unless you're spoken to." Though that seemed strange, Deirdre had to accept that Mrs. Gansworthy knew more about manners than she did; after all, Mum didn't have dinner parties. But the twins, Elizabeth and Patience, were brats and talked out of turn all through the meal, and everyone thought they were cute. Mrs. Gansworthy was even smiling at them! Deirdre simmered with resentment.

Afterward, when Deirdre was in bed, she could hear the dishes clattering as the cook and Abigail cleaned up downstairs.

And, much later, she heard the Gansworthys talking.

"It went well, don't you think?" Mrs. Gansworthy said.

"Splendidly. You outdid yourself with that apple pie," Reverend Gansworthy said. "Martha Wenner said it was the flakiest she'd ever...And at the door, Dr. Peters said you were a saint..."

Mrs. Gansworthy's voice, almost girlish: "Dr. Peters said that to you?"

"...caring for that girl...she struck him as very quiet and gloomy."

"Well, that's the truth!" Mrs. Gansworthy's voice. "...always underfoot...too quiet and secretive...I never know what she's thinking."

"...obligation..." Reverend Gansworthy cleared his throat. "...we agreed to..."

Mrs. Gansworthy's voice rose. "...and Miss Harrow says...incorrigible..."

"It's difficult but...and the congregation is well aware..."

"I know, I know, the congregation! You're always the fine one, but the burden falls on me!"

"Margaret, for years you wanted a child, and I thought—"

"I wanted a baby of my own, not someone else's mistake!" Her words came out harsh and bitter. "I accepted that I wasn't blessed, and I had everything in order, and then you spring this on me! You thought! You didn't ask me, did you? Well, any daughter *I* raised would be entirely different! Miss Harrow told me..."

Deirdre cringed under her blanket.

"No, I wasn't blessed, but those women drop one baby after another and think nothing of giving them away. Like animals."

Deirdre bolted upright in bed. What a terrible, mean thing to say!

A picture of Mum at that last moment came into her mind. Mum, walking stiff-legged and fast toward the corner, with her arms wrapped tight around her body, wrapped as if she had to hold herself together. Deirdre suddenly realized—it did matter to Mum, Mum was *hurting,* that's what it was! It was hard for her to give them away! Deirdre wished she could ask her, just ask why. But whatever the reason, she and Jimmy and Sean weren't worthless.

"Maybe with time and patience—" Reverend Gansworthy started.

"You expect too much of me! I can't make a silk purse out of a sow's ear."

A sow's ear. They were calling her a sow's ear! Deirdre's

head buzzed with fury. They were wrong, she was as good as anyone! She was so mad that tears sprang to her eyes. The Gansworthys had made her feel ashamed of herself—well, they were the ones who ought to be ashamed! Because they had tight, tiny hearts. With all their church talk and smugness and fancy ways, they were nothing but fakes. All this time, she'd been smothering herself, trying to please people who couldn't be pleased! No more. She was no sow's ear! She'd been too timid and meek. Sean would have fought back from the first day.

She couldn't stay in this house, Deirdre thought. She could leave the Gansworthys without a backward glance, and they'd be just as glad to see her go. She had to get away from this place, and she needed Sean's help. Why didn't he come for her?... Maybe he couldn't. Maybe he was trapped somewhere. It suddenly struck Deirdre—her big brother was just a kid himself, not that much older; he wasn't a grownup with power and money any more than she was. Here she'd been waiting and waiting for Sean to rescue her; maybe it was up to her to find him.

She couldn't remember where that boy Aloysius had said the orphan train would be stopping. She wished she'd listened better. Pennsylvania...Kansas...going west...No matter how hard she tried, she couldn't remember past that.

Deirdre woke up the next morning with an idea. It wasn't a real plan yet, but she had to do something to try to find Sean. She felt stronger than anytime since she'd been in

Greenville. In a whisper, she sang, "There's a change in the weather, there's a change in the sea, and from now on there'll be a change in me..." Why was she whisper-singing anyway? She could belt that great Sophie Tucker song, and why should she care if Mrs. Gansworthy heard her?

"I'm gonna change my way of living and if that ain't enough
I'll even change the way I strut my stuff..."

She wasn't a red-hot mama like Sophie Tucker, but her voice was back, true and strong and bouncing off the walls. It gave her courage, and she felt that old joy running through her.

"Nothing about me's gonna be the same
There'll be some changes made today."

She felt more free than she had in a long time, and she gathered her breath for the big finish.

"There'll be some changes made!"

When she came downstairs, Mrs. Gansworthy frowned. "Exactly what was that racket? What got into you?"

"Nothing that ain't been there all along," Deirdre said. She'd never talked back before. It was a whole lot better to be bad than to feel pathetic.

She waited until the ticket booth would be open for the five-thirty train. Then she headed to the railroad station.

"Excuse me, sir," she said to the ticket man. "I need to know about the train."

"Going on a trip, little miss?" He put his paper down and smiled at her.

"Um—no, not yet—but where does the five-thirty go after Greenville?" She had arrived in Greenville in the evening, she remembered that much.

"Smith Center, Sharon Springs, Salt Lake City… Where do you want to go?" He looked at her more closely. "Say, aren't you that little orphan girl staying with the minister and his wife?"

Her heart stopped. "Yes, sir," she said. If the Gansworthys heard she was searching for Sean, they'd stop her!

"Fine people, the Gansworthys. You're lucky to—"

"It's—it's for a report for school," she said quickly. "About where the trains go and schedules and…and where they go from here."

"Well, you can get anywhere in the U.S. of A. from Greenville, what do you think of that?" he said proudly. "As far as Texas and Californ-i-ay if you make the right connections. The midnight train goes to Topeka and…Denver and…You can change to the Atchison, Topeka and Santa Fe, it's all connected, you see. Now, if a body had a mind to go to Phoenix…"

Deirdre listened in despair as he rattled off the names.

"Here's some schedules for you to study. If you get an A on that report, you come back and let me know."

Deirdre nodded; her throat felt too tight to speak. Her shoulders sagged as she wandered along the paving near the tracks. She wouldn't worry about getting in trouble, she'd do anything at all, if she knew where to search. She was dizzy with all those names: Topeka, Denver, Santa Fe. Big and little towns in between. She didn't think there would be so many, it was too hard, she didn't even know where to start.

She watched the five-thirty come into the station. Only a few people got on and hardly any got off; not much doing in Greenville. Then the stationmaster waved, the whistle blew, and the train chugged away.

Deirdre's eyes followed the tracks until they got smaller and disappeared at the horizon. Where was Sean? There was no clue at all, just miles and miles of brown and yellow fields as far as she could see.

FOURTEEN

Deirdre trudged from school back to the Gansworthys' house under a gray December sky that threatened snow. Her breath made puffs of smoke in the air. Winter in Kansas was colder than any she'd known.

Deirdre fumbled through her mittens with the front doorknob. The freezing wind cut against her cheeks. It crept up her coat sleeves and made her shiver. Even the bare black trees seemed to draw into themselves, limbs cracking with frost. Deirdre thought she'd never get warm enough.

Abigail poked her head into the hallway when Deirdre came in.

"Letter for you," Abigail said. She held up an envelope. "Says 'Texas' on the return address. You know somebody in Texas?"

"I don't know," Deirdre said. She held her breath; could she dare hope—? "Give it to me."

"Don't grab!" Abigail handed the envelope over reluctantly.

It said DEIRDRE O'ROURKE—in Sean's handwriting! Unless she was just wishing too hard...No, it looked neater than it used to, but—it *was* Sean's handwriting! The envelope shook in Deirdre's hand.

"Ain't you gonna open it?" Abigail asked. "Who's it from?"

Deirdre ran upstairs to her room, away from Abigail's prying eyes. She tore at the flap with trembling fingers. She tried to take in all the words at once and some of them blurred and she read them over and over again:

Dear Deirdre,

I wrote you 3 letters over at the Andersons, I got your address from the agent soon as the train pulled out of Greenville. Anyway, I wrote 3 letters but you didn't ~~anser~~ answer none of them. So I got worried, so I wrote to Children's Aid in NYC and they sent me your new address. What happened with the Andersons?

I got Jimmy's address and his people wrote back to me. They said he's doing well and he's happy. They said they love him.

I asked Children's Aid for Mum's address, but they said we're supposed to make a clean break. I don't think they know where she's at anyway, so I'm not that mad at them. They'll help brothers and sisters stay in touch though.

It's good here. Pop Roy says I'm good with horses—

bet you're surprised! Mom Lorene helps me catch up in school, ~~especialy~~ especially spelling. I'm taking their name, so write back to Sean Langford. Write back quick.

Your brother,

Sean Langford

Deirdre's emotions tumbled on top of each other and left her breathless, mostly with pure joy. Sean hadn't forgotten about her! Now she knew where he was! She knew where to find him—it was right there on the paper! Box 545, R.R. 1, Bandera, Texas!

But—Sean Langford? Were they making him change his name, and how come he wasn't fighting back? And what was that Pop Roy—a name for soda pop!—and Mom Lorene? That didn't sound like Sean at all.

It was good that Jimmy was happy and had a new family to love him, but—he was so little, he'd forget everything about her and Sean and their life together in no time. She felt like she was losing him all over again.

And she was so mad at herself! If she'd known she could get Sean's address from Children's Aid, she could have written to him right at the beginning! She'd never thought to ask somebody. She'd wasted all this time pining away, for nothing!

But none of that mattered anymore. She ran her fingers over Sean's handwriting. He hadn't abandoned her! He was in Bandera, Texas, and somehow, someway, she would get there!

Deirdre wrote back to Sean right away. She curled up on her bed with a pencil and her copybook.

December 2, 1927

Dear Sean,

I miss you. I'm happy you found me and sent a letter. Now I know where you're at so I feel lots better. I want to get to Bandera, Texas and be with you. Where's Bandera? I can't find it on the map in the atlas.

In school, Deirdre didn't like writing. Her penmanship was no good, and she wasn't used to writing in ink. Miss Harrow frowned if she made splatters when she dipped her pen in the inkwell. And sometimes the nib of the pen split—she couldn't help it! She never knew what to say in the compositions: "How I Spent My Summer" or "How to Prevent Forest Fires." She'd leave most of the page blank, and Miss Harrow didn't expect anything more from her.

But a letter to Sean was different. Her pencil flew across the page. Now she had someone to talk to, even if only on paper. Everything inside spilled over into words and more words.

Everyone here hates me. My teacher and all the kids hate me. I don't have a single friend and nobody to play with. Except for my collie, Rex. He's not really my dog but he acts like it. He's the only thing I like here. The people I'm staying with don't like me neither. They feed me good, but I don't care. I don't care about none of them. I hate Greenville, Kansas and I want to get rid of it real soon.

Deirdre wrote on and on. She felt almost as if Sean was there, listening. She covered three pages, until the pencil point wore down to nothing. Stopping to look for the sharpener broke the spell. And then she knew she could never send the letter to Sean, though putting it all down made her feel better. What was the point of worrying him when he couldn't do anything for her from a distance? No, she'd wait to tell him about Greenville in person, when it was all over. When she'd already made her way to Texas.

She rewrote the first paragraph on clean paper and added:

I'm okay for now. I saw The Jazz Singer. Did you? Write soon.

That's what she mailed to him.

Sean's answer was only a couple of sentences, and she wondered if he was holding back the bad stuff, too.

The nearest city to Bandera is Austin. We don't live right in Bandera, we're a little ways outside. Things are good here. The Langfords ain't rich and there's no extra for movies, but we've got horses and land. Write back soon.

Well, then, Deirdre thought, he won't be able to pay my way to Texas, that's for sure. I'll have to get there on my own. Once we're together, we can figure out what to do next.

• • •

In school, everyone was talking about the vaudeville show coming to the Victoria. Vaudeville came through town just twice a year, in May and December, and everyone was excited about it.

The other kids were making plans about whom they'd go with, and Deirdre was left out again. She tried not to care so much.

"In New York," Deirdre said, "there's vaudeville all the time, all over, lots of places and not just twice a year!" She wasn't trying to be nice and humble anymore; she'd be gone soon, and she'd never have to see any of their faces again. "Downtown there's the Variety and the Columbia and Tony Pastor's and the National and lots more, and uptown the Palace and the Ziegfeld Follies and—"

Frances rolled her eyes. "And you went to all those?"

"Some of them. And not only in May and December, either!"

At the Variety and the Columbia, all of Sean's friends would chip in to buy one ticket; one boy would go in regular admission and then sneak around to the back and open the fire door for the others. Deirdre saw plenty of shows at the Variety when Sean took her along. They were wonderful, with tap dancers and magicians and singers in spangled dresses! The Columbia was sleazy, full of cigar smoke and chorus girls dressed in almost nothing and dancing out of step, but she'd have gone anyplace at all to see vaudeville. Then after a while, the managers got wise; the Variety had ushers watching the fire doors, and the Columbia locked them from the inside. Sean was indignant. "That's against the law!" She could almost hear his voice. Remembering those days made her ache.

Tony Pastor's was one of the best places—they called it clean family entertainment—but it was impossible to sneak in there. The Palace and the Ziegfeld Follies had the biggest stars—Eddie Cantor, Fanny Brice, Sophie Tucker, Al Jolson, and the glamorous Ziegfeld girls in millions of dollars' worth of feathers and sequins! That's where they had stage-door johnnies and limousines waiting at the stage entrance. Not that she'd ever seen that herself; she never went uptown, that was like a separate country.

Deirdre wondered what the vaudeville show at the Victoria would be like. Oh, she wanted to see it! But she'd never ask the Gansworthys for money. She wouldn't ask them for anything. Anyway, if she had money, she'd save it for train fare.

During free time, when all the other kids were buzzing with plans for going to the Victoria, Deirdre studied the big map of the United States on the back wall. Okay, there was Texas in yellow with an extra-big dot for Austin because it was the state capital, but Bandera wasn't on this map, either. Texas was much too far away! Greenville was all the way at the top of Kansas, north of Topeka, and Texas was down at the bottom of the map, with all of Oklahoma in between! There was no way but the train.

Deirdre was sizzling with energy; she'd move mountains to be with Sean again, so surely she could come up with the fare. She'd always made money singing, hadn't she?

After school, Deirdre looked for a good place. In front of a speakeasy was always best, but there weren't any in Greenville, at least as far as she could tell. So she picked a busy spot on Main Street, in front of the five-and-dime. Back home, she'd used a man's hat to catch the coins, but that was left behind someplace on Division Street. She put her jacket on the ground in front of her and carefully rolled up the edges. It would have to do. She put two nickels on it to get things started. A passerby glanced at her curiously.

She went into the first line of "April Showers." Her voice came out thin and wispy. She felt too uncomfortable in Greenville. She took a deep breath and started over. Pretend you're on the street outside Gallagher's, she told herself, with car horns honking and the smell of beer and smoke drifting from the doorway. Her voice rang out with "Bye, Bye, Blackbird."

A few people stopped, and then some others. She smiled at them as she sang, but no one smiled back. They were staring at her in an odd way. It didn't feel right.

"What's happening here?" a man's voice asked.

"It's the reverend's ward. I think she's trying to beg!"

Deirdre faltered to the end of the song. No one clapped. No coins rang down. There was an awful silence.

"Does Mrs. Gansworthy know what you're up to?" a woman asked indignantly.

Deirdre felt the heat rise in her face as she stooped to

pick up her jacket. She brushed it off and avoided their eyes. She wanted to run, but she made herself walk away. She could feel them staring at her back. Everything I do here turns out wrong, she thought—everything! I can't wait to leave this place!

When she entered the house, Mrs. Gansworthy was waiting in the hallway. Her furious expression told Deirdre that she had already heard all about it. Deirdre tried to go by, but Mrs. Gansworthy grabbed her arm.

"Exactly what did you think you were doing?" There were bright red spots on Mrs. Gansworthy's cheeks. "Making a public spectacle of yourself! And us! Begging on Main Street! Were you *trying* to shame us?"

"I was trying to work, that's all, doing what I know how." There was no shame in an honest day's work, Deirdre thought. Mum had taught her that.

"What's wrong with you? Don't we feed you enough? Don't we clothe you? Everyone's talking about it! I've never been so humiliated!"

The only shame was in taking grudging handouts, Deirdre thought. She held her head up. She had somewhere to go; she was somebody.

"And with everything we've done for you!" Mrs. Gansworthy stared at her. "Is that what you come from? A bunch of beggars?"

"Back home, people liked my singing and they gave me money 'cause I entertained them. I call that working," Deirdre said, but that just set Mrs. Gansworthy off some more.

She went on and on, yelling, "If it's work you want, take out the garbage. And dust your room! You should be showing gratitude instead of—"

Deirdre stopped listening. Everything in her was pointed toward Texas now.

When the reverend came home, Mrs. Gansworthy told him, spitting out the words.

"And what do you have to say for yourself, young lady?" he asked.

Deirdre raised her chin and looked him right in the eye. "Where I come from, there's no harm in earning your money. It's sloth that's a deadly sin."

"Well," Reverend Gansworthy said. "Well. The child doesn't know any better. I can see she doesn't understand. Maybe with time and patience—maybe you're being a bit hard on her, Margaret."

Mrs. Gansworthy glared at him.

"Now, let's back up," Reverend Gansworthy said. "Why do you want money? What were you planning to buy?"

Deirdre was stumped. There was a pause. A too-long pause.

And then a reason finally popped into her head. "The vaudeville show is coming to the Victoria. I wanted to buy a ticket."

That seemed to satisfy him, and he didn't ask any more questions.

Deirdre couldn't help it; as the days went by, she started thinking about Mrs. Gansworthy's pocketbook. There was money in it, for sure. Mostly, Mrs. Gansworthy took it into her bedroom; sometimes she left it on the sideboard in the dining room.

That was stealing.

But she had to get to Texas. If she took the money and ran away, she'd be long gone before anyone found out…

She had never stolen before. Well, she'd swiped an apple from Giambelli's fruit stand, but she'd done it only once, with her heart hammering like anything. Sean had done it lots of times—apples and bananas, too.

She had to get to Sean! She'd steal only this one time…

Stealing the Gansworthys' money was lots worse than swiping an apple. She'd be a real thief. The Gansworthys would know that about her. Miss Harrow would know, too. And Deirdre could almost hear them all saying, "Well, what did you expect?"

That was the truth, that's exactly what they would expect of her. So she couldn't go and prove them right.

There had to be some other way of getting train fare. There had to be.

FIFTEEN

9 WORLD-FAMOUS ACTS 9! the banner in front of the Victoria screamed in red and yellow. The vaudeville show would be in town for only two days, Friday and Saturday. Deirdre wished with all her heart that she could see it. At dinner on Friday, she listened to the Gansworthys talk about it.

"It's not the same group that passed through in June, is it?" Mrs. Gansworthy said. "Allstate Variety—they bill themselves as clean family entertainment."

"Yes, but you never know with those showfolk." Reverend Gansworthy took a sip of coffee. "Most of the town is going—women and children, too. If it's anything less than appropriate, I hope my flock walks out immediately."

"It wouldn't hurt to take a look, would it?" Mrs. Gansworthy asked. "It's something to do…"

"Hmm. Maybe tomorrow afternoon."

Mrs. Gansworthy turned to Deirdre. "Obviously, you want to go. Very badly, indeed."

Deirdre held her breath. Did that mean they might take her?

"Singing on the street like an urchin! All for the price of a ticket," Mrs. Gansworthy continued.

"Don't start again, Margaret. The child meant no harm. She didn't know any better."

"Deirdre, you need to understand why I was so upset." Mrs. Gansworthy sighed. "A minister's family has a special position, and it can be difficult. People watch every single thing we do and say. And they're very quick to criticize and start rumors. Maybe, with your background, begging seemed like a natural thing to do. But you could start people talking that we're depriving you. Now, you're not deprived of anything here, are you?"

Deirdre shrugged.

Mrs. Gansworthy gave her a stern look. "If you wanted to go that much, wouldn't it make sense to simply ask us?"

"I guess," Deirdre said. *I wouldn't ask you for anything,* she thought, *not in a million years.*

"And you've been sassing me all week," Mrs. Gansworthy continued.

"I'm sure she'll try to be good," Reverend Gansworthy said. "She's not really a bad girl."

Reverend Gansworthy was the kinder one, Deirdre thought, but he always talked about her as if she wasn't sitting right there.

"All right, you may come along on Saturday," Mrs.

Gansworthy said, "if I can expect to see a big change in your attitude."

She was going! She was going to the show!

After dinner on Friday, Reverend Gansworthy was feeling poorly with a chill. On Saturday morning, he sounded hoarse. "I have to cure this scratchy throat, get my voice in shape for tomorrow's sermon," he said. He went back to bed right after breakfast. "I don't feel up to the Victoria."

Deirdre sagged with disappointment.

But later Mrs. Gansworthy said, "Honestly, the whole house smells of camphor. I can't bear much more of this!"

She was taking Deirdre to the show, after all!

Most of the seats in the theater were already filled when they entered. This time the movie screen was rolled up, and there in plain view was the stage, the very place where she and Sean had been put on display. Deirdre tried to blot out the shamed, lost feeling that came flooding back.

There was an excited buzz. It looked as if all of Greenville had turned out. Mrs. Gansworthy led Deirdre to seats near the back.

Three rows ahead, Deirdre saw Norma, Doris, and Gwendolyn. Their heads were together, and they were talking and giggling.

Deirdre looked at Mrs. Gansworthy's stern face and wished she had friends to sit with. She felt so all alone.

But the piano started—*da-da-da-dum, da-da, da-da,* good-time music, ragtime. And then the band joined in! It made Deirdre's heart bounce. A real live vaudeville show!

A deep voice announced, "Ladies and gentlemen, for your entertainment pleasure, direct from Shanghai—THE AMAZING PING BROTHERS!" Three men in tights took the stage. Deirdre watched in wonder as they juggled balls and hoops and then flaming torches! And—oops—they almost dropped one but caught it just in time. People were still coming into the theater and walking up the aisles. Deirdre had to crane her neck around them to see it all.

A man changed a card at the side of the stage. It said TRIXIE DEE with a lot of curlicues. Trixie Dee was a fat lady with a ukulele. She sang a song about Hannah doing the hula-hula in Hawaii. It was funny, too, because Hannah fell on her hula-hula-behind. Deirdre glanced at Mrs. Gansworthy. She was frowning at that line, just as Deirdre knew she would be. So Deirdre clapped extra-hard when Trixie Dee took her bow.

The next card said THE GREAT REGURGITATOR. There was a drumroll as a man in tails and a top hat came on stage.

"What's a regurgitator?" Deirdre whispered.

Mrs. Gansworthy raised her eyebrows. "Regurgitate means to throw up."

"Like vomit?" Deirdre didn't think she wanted to see that. But his act was great! He lit a toy house on fire and the flames shot up so high that everyone gasped. Then he stepped back with a flourish and swallowed two big glasses of water. From a distance, he spewed the water out in powerful arcs, aiming right at the house. He was exactly like a fire hose! When the flames went out, everyone applauded.

The new card said THE SIX SANTINIS, and the voice announced, "The comedy toast-a of New York-a: THE SIX SANTINIS!" Three kids and two grownups ran out. A girl stood in front, singing a song about going back to old Napoli. Behind her, the rest of them were acting out her words, pretending to row across the ocean and bumping into each other and doing pratfalls and yelling in broken English. It looked like there were a lot of them all over the stage. But when Deirdre counted, there were only five. She was puzzled—there were supposed to be six Santinis, weren't there?

"Ladies and gentlemen, presenting the international star—ROSIE FRANCE!" Rosie France had long, curly red hair, and she wore a green satin gown. She was glamorous! She had on a big green picture hat with shamrocks all over it. She stood in the middle of the stage with her hands on her hips and her chin up, and she sang, "I'm the Daughter of Rosie O'Grady."

Deirdre was full of pride in Rosie France. She'd bet anything Rosie really was the daughter of Rosie O'Grady, Irish through and through.

Rosie France's eyes gleamed and she smiled mischievously. "You ain't seen nothing yet!" She said it even more sassy than Jolson. And she went into "When Irish Eyes Are Smiling." One of Deirdre's songs!

Mum said it wasn't truly Irish, it was a Tin Pan Alley song, but Deirdre liked it. She couldn't help mouthing the words along with Rosie. It felt as if they were singing together.

Between verses, Rosie had a few words of patter for the audience. And the way she pronounced the words was so familiar to Deirdre. She spoke exactly like somebody from the city, from home! Deirdre hoped Norma, Doris, and Gwendolyn noticed; they couldn't make fun of the way she talked anymore, could they? Not when Rosie France, an international star, talked the very same way.

Then the music speeded up into something else that didn't sound Irish at all, and Rosie did a whole lot of cancan kicks! Her underpants showed—they were green satin, too. She twirled her dress so you could see way past her knees, and she winked at the audience. Mrs. Gansworthy muttered, "Vulgar."

But Deirdre thought Rosie France was great! She could sing and *dance,* too! There were lots of whistles and applause when she took a bow.

In the lobby, at intermission, Mrs. Gansworthy didn't look happy. "This was supposed to be family fare," she said. "Well, what can you expect from show people!"

"They didn't do anything bad," Deirdre said. "They were wonderful."

Mrs. Gansworthy looked at her sharply. "I don't think you can be the judge of that."

Deirdre was afraid that Mrs. Gansworthy would make them leave, and she wanted to see the rest of the show so much! But maybe Mrs. Gansworthy did, too, because she led the way back to their seats.

Deirdre was spellbound as the rest of the show

unfurled. A whole bunch of cute poodles doing tricks, and then two funny men with German accents. Then came Charlie Morgan, a man with a straw hat and a cane, singing "Waiting for the *Robert E. Lee.*" He tap-danced across the stage with an infectious smile, so confident and breezy, twirling his hat and singing all the way. He made Deirdre want to go right down to the levee, like he said—whatever a levee was. Everyone clapped along with the beat of the catchy song—even Mrs. Gansworthy was smiling.

It all went by too fast. The very last act was a boy riding a unicycle. That was a letdown, but Deirdre still felt the glow.

On the way out, Mrs. Gansworthy received respectful greetings, and a group clustered around her.

"Mostly slapstick," Mrs. Gansworthy said. "I sat through it for Deirdre's sake. The poor child never saw a show before."

"Aren't you a lucky girl!" Mrs. Truett smiled at Deirdre. "You must be thrilled to be in a lovely home and—"

Deirdre nodded automatically and shut out the rest of her words. She blinked in the daylight and fidgeted as Mrs. Gansworthy and the women chatted in front of the theater.

"—and not a bit cultural or uplifting," Mrs. Gansworthy was saying. "A ragtag band of gypsies. Did you see that Rosie France doing the cancan? That's when I thought about leaving."

Mrs. Judson clucked in agreement, but then she said, "You've got to admit that Charlie Morgan sure lights up a stage."

"All right, he's the best of the lot," Mrs. Gansworthy answered.

"They tried to check in at the hotel," Mrs. Cartwright said. "But no, sir, Allen Dunhill wouldn't let them. He knows about showfolk coming through, stealing towels and whatnot."

"Anything that's not nailed down," Mrs. Hodgkins added. "So they're all staying at the rooming house."

"Mildred says showfolk or not, their money's welcome as far as she's concerned. Mind you, she's charging them a pretty penny."

Maybe people didn't think much of vaudeville folk off stage, Deirdre thought, but on stage, they shone and sparkled. It looked like they had fun showing off because they could perform in such spectacular ways. Look at how Charlie Morgan tap-danced and threw his cane high and caught it and sang, all at the same time! They took control; they could make people clap and laugh and admire and beg for more. Rosie France, Trixie Dee, all of them—they were glamorous and glittering and larger than life!

Deirdre remembered how she'd been picked over and examined like a thing on sale at an auction. An unwilling thing, smaller than life, with no control over what would happen to her. She'd stood on the same stage, she thought, but it was entirely different. Today it was wonderful; she wished she could watch Rosie France and Charlie Morgan forever!

The women kept on chattering, and Deirdre wandered

from the group. She checked out a poster in front of the theater. ALLSTATE VARIETY EXTRAVAGANZA! she read. Underneath, there was a photo of Charlie Morgan in his straw hat.

Mrs. Gansworthy was still talking. Deirdre was restless. She went to check the billboard at the other side of the entrance. She read COMING TO A TOWN NEAR YOU! TWO DAYS ONLY! THREE BIG SHOWS A DAY! Bored, Deirdre skimmed the list of dates and towns. Altoona, October 8 and 9, South Bend...Peoria...Dubuque...Greenville, December 15 and 16. That was today. Topeka, Fort Collins, Denver...Fort Worth, Houston, Galveston! They were traveling on to Texas!

Deirdre had a sudden rush of blood that left her weak-kneed. Right there, in front of her nose, was the answer to her prayers!

SIXTEEN

Fort Worth, Houston, Galveston! Deirdre stared at the billboard. She had to tag along somehow!

"Come along, Deirdre. Don't dawdle," Mrs. Gansworthy called. The group of women around her had scattered.

The last show was tonight, and then they'd be gone!

"Deirdre!"

Stragglers were still coming through the door.

"I'm waiting—um—for some girls from my class to come out." Deirdre went toward Mrs. Gansworthy. "Can I play with them until dinner?"

"May I," Mrs. Gansworthy said.

"May I?" Deirdre repeated. Her heart was beating double-time. "Please?"

"I'm glad you found someone to play with instead of that dog." Mrs. Gansworthy glanced at her watch. "All right, you have about an hour. But don't be late. Six-thirty prompt, washed up and at the table, and not a minute later."

"Yes, ma'am."

Deirdre's mind raced as she watched Mrs. Gansworthy walk down Main Street. Rosie France—she was the one to talk to. Hadn't she felt a special kinship with Rosie, with her Irish song and her New York speech? But—how should she ask? What words to use...? How would she get inside? In a Gloria Swanson movie, there'd been a door marked STAGE with millionaires' limousines parked in front and a guard on the other side. What if she couldn't get in? She had to! She'd beg the guard and...

Deirdre waited until Mrs. Gansworthy turned the corner. Then she scooted around the side of the theater. Maple Street was as quiet as ever and not a limousine to be seen anywhere.

Finally, Deirdre found a dented steel door facing the alley behind the Victoria. But it didn't say anything on it. Deirdre knocked hesitantly. No answer. She knocked harder. Nothing. She turned the knob, and the door opened with a squeak into a narrow hallway. Deirdre took a moment to adjust to the dim light. What now? Nowhere to go but up a short flight of stairs.

She barely had a foot on the first step when she was stopped short by an explosion of voices. Mostly a man's rough voice.

"Six Santinis! *Six!* That's how we booked you!"

"Just until Tina comes back—" A woman's voice.

"Well, the act ain't funny!" The rough voice again. "Not enough tummeling goin' on behind the canary!"

"We got laughs!" A different man's voice, also yelling.

There was a chorus of high-pitched barking, and the rough voice shouted over it, "You're getting pay for six!"

"More like for two and a half!" the other man exploded.

"You got a problem, take it up with the office," the rough voice said. "I'm telling you, it ain't funny. I oughta put you in the last spot."

"Over my dead body! The Santinis don't play to the haircuts!"

Deirdre couldn't make sense of anything she was hearing.

"Then make the act move. Fix it, and fast, for tonight's show," the rough voice said. "Okay, I'll meet up with all of youse in Denver."

Before Deirdre could get out of the way, a heavy man in a double-breasted wide-striped suit came charging down the stairs. She was scared, but he brushed by her without a second glance and slammed out.

The barking continued, along with a murmur of voices. Deirdre followed the sounds to the top of the stairs and down another hall. She stopped in the doorway of a room, too bright with bare light bulbs dangling from the ceiling. The people crowded in it had orange faces! She smelled sweat and something waxy; she didn't know what that was. The room was ice-cold, freezing, but there seemed to be steam rising from all those people. Then Deirdre spotted long red hair. She could see only the back of her head, but that had to be Rosie France sitting in front of the mirror!

Five little dogs were running in circles, still barking.

Gosh, they were the performing poodles she'd seen on the stage.

And Rosie France, right here, in person! Deirdre looked everywhere at once, dazzled and confused. That man over there, wasn't he the biggest Santini? He was bare-chested, and in mixed company, too. The orange stuff on his face stopped with a stripe below his neck.

"...and we need to get the action going double-time," he was saying.

"Papa, I can't somersault faster," a boy whined.

"We'll work on it. Find a way to fill more of the stage. You heard Bremer, we better get started."

"Tina shouldna left," a little voice said. "That was so bad, right, Papa?"

The poodles yipped.

"Can't you shut them up?" It was the unicycle boy! He was standing on his head with his feet resting against the wall. Stacks of film reels and boxes were piled up near him.

"No, I can't!" the poodle lady snapped. "They're sensitive, and that s.o.b. upset them."

"At least Bremer shows up when he's supposed to. Ever been stranded?" a fat lady said. "In '23, the whole troupe was stuck in Paducah without a cent. Me, I'm happy when the manager shows up."

The fat lady was Trixie Dee! Instead of her hula-hula skirt, she was wearing a faded kimono. It was tied loosely, and her whole slip showed! She noticed Deirdre standing on the threshold. "Looking for something?"

Suddenly everyone was staring at Deirdre.

"Go to the box office, girlie," Trixie Dee said. Without her ukulele, she didn't act the least bit jolly. "This is private quarters here."

"Excuse me, but—" Deirdre gathered her courage. "I need to talk to Rosie France. It's important."

That's when Rosie France turned around. She was wiping grease off her face with a tissue. Her face was bare of makeup and very shiny. She was no more than a teenager! And instead of the glamorous green satin gown, she was wearing an oversized man's shirt, with her elbow sticking out of a hole in the sleeve. The shirt covered her only down to her bare thighs. Deirdre couldn't help staring, shocked. Rosie France's eyelashes were light reddish, hardly there. What happened to the long, sweeping dark lashes that Deirdre remembered?

Rosie looked at her curiously. "Well, what do you want?"

This wasn't at all the way Deirdre had imagined it. "Can we—can we talk privately?" she asked. "Like—like in your dressing room?"

Rosie laughed. "This is it, kid."

Deirdre couldn't believe it. In the movie, Gloria Swanson's dressing room was beautiful and filled with flowers from the stage-door johnnies. Wasn't Rosie France, an international star, supposed to have her own dressing room with a big star on the door?

"Well, what is it?" Rosie asked.

Deirdre didn't know how to start in front of all those people. She shifted awkwardly and looked at the peeling walls and the water stains. A gurgling pipe along the wall was leaking. "I just—I just wanted to ask you…" Her voice trailed off.

"Cat got your tongue?" Rosie said, smiling. She stood up. "Come on, we can go out in the hall."

Deirdre followed her. "I saw you in the show this afternoon. You were so wonderful! I clapped and clapped until my hands hurt!"

"Well, thanks." Rosie stopped at the top of the stairs. "Okay, what is it you want? You don't have to be so shy. You want my autograph?"

"Sure, but—" Deirdre took a breath. "The thing is, I want to go along with the show. To Texas. I need to. And if you'd—"

"So that's it!" Rosie shook her head. "Yeah, I know, everyone wants to run away with the circus." She leaned on the banister. "What happened? Your mom punish you for something and you're mad at her? Go on home, it'll blow over."

"I don't *have* a home," Deirdre said, and tears suddenly threatened to well up. Embarrassed, she swallowed them. "I thought you'd help me. Being Irish and all, and from New York like me. I used to live on Division, well, first on Rivington, and then—and my name's Deirdre O'Rourke, and I need to go with you, I'd do anything, work my way and—"

"Well, you got the New York part right—Delancey

124

Street—but my real name's Francie Rosen. Not exactly Irish."

"But the shamrocks! And 'The Daughter of Rosie O'Grady'!"

Rosie shrugged. "That's show business."

Deirdre clutched at an idea. "My mum came from Connemara, and I know a million real Irish songs! I can sing! I could—"

Rosie's eyes turned cold. "Forget it, kid. I'm the only colleen act in this show. And I work alone."

"Oh." Deirdre knew she'd made a mistake, but she wasn't sure what it was. This wasn't turning out right. She was losing Rosie France. Or Francie Rosen. Or whoever.

The poodle lady went by with the dogs, each on a separate leash but amazingly untangled. "Taking the ladies out for a run," she said as they trotted down the stairs and out the door.

"I could walk the dogs," Deirdre said. "I'd take care of them and clean them and—I'm real good with dogs and—"

"Gloria can't afford a dog-walker. Look, I don't have much time before the next show, so—" Rosie was turning away.

"I'd do it for nothing. If I can just go on the train with you and—" Deirdre found herself talking to Rosie's back.

"Train fare and room and board, that all costs," Rosie threw over her shoulder. She was walking toward the dressing room.

"I don't have to eat until Texas. I promise, I wouldn't eat anything at all." Deirdre followed her in despair. "I'd sleep anywhere, I don't care, I've slept out on the street before. Please, this is my only chance. *Please*."

Rosie looked at Deirdre long and hard. "Chance for what? What's in Texas?"

And then Deirdre blurted out everything, everything spilling out at once, the orphan train, and the Gansworthys and Miss Harrow and the vomit stain on Norma's used dress and Jimmy and Sean—most of all, Sean!

When she finished, she was breathless. There was a long silence.

Finally, Rosie broke it with a sigh. "Sometimes life stinks. I have a running-from-home story of my own," she said.

"You do? Were they mean to you at home?"

Rosie shook her head. "No, nothing like that. My papa was wonderful. I was his favorite, and I broke his heart. But I had to leave…" A shadow fell across Rosie's face. Deirdre waited for her to go on.

"Maybe I'll tell you sometime." Rosie straightened up. "The thing is, everyone in the show does something, you know? There's no extra for dressers or—" She seemed deep in thought. "How old are you anyway?"

Deirdre took a breath. "Sixteen?" The truth was, she'd grown a lot taller; she'd been growing out of her clothes.

Rosie laughed. "Sure. You're sixteen the way I'm twenty-one." She looked Deirdre over. "I guess we could say fourteen. If we stretch it a bit."

"You'll help me?" Deirdre asked breathlessly. "Will you?"

"I don't know." Rosie scratched her neck. "Your hair's dark enough, you could pass…" She seemed to be talking to herself.

"I'm a hard worker," Deirdre said. "I am."

"Hmm, maybe…Was that true, can you sing a little?"

Quick, before she lost Rosie again, Deirdre started on "Bye, Bye, Blackbird." She sang as loudly and clearly as she could, as if her life depended on it.

Her singing pulled some of the people out of the dressing room. They clustered in the doorway, listening.

"Tina Santini took off with the drummer," Rosie whispered. "They've got Marie doing the song now, but they need her carrying on upstage with the others…" She turned to the group in the doorway. "Hey, I found you a new Santini!"

"What?" Mrs. Santini took a step forward. "Who is she?"

"Look, she's here and she sings well enough, don't she?" Rosie said. "A gift for you, dropped right out of the sky."

"She's got a good set of pipes," the unicycle boy put in.

"Maybe. I don't know," Mrs. Santini said. "What about her folks?"

"Don't worry about them." Rosie spoke quickly before Deirdre could say anything. "They gave permission already. They want her in a show. She's got a stage mother—her mother sent her here—but, thank goodness, Mom'll stay home. This trip anyway."

Mr. Santini had been listening over Mrs. Santini's shoulder. "She looks all right. What do you think? We could break her in on the way to Topeka…"

The Santinis didn't have a trace of the accent they used on the stage. Nothing in vaudeville was what it seemed, Deirdre thought.

"I don't know," Mrs. Santini said. "Tina might—"

"She won't. We need a replacement, and you know it." Mr. Santini turned to Deirdre. "You've seen the act?"

Deirdre nodded quickly. "This afternoon." She added, "It was real good."

"She could work out," Mr. Santini said. "Six Santinis. Six, Irene."

"Possible—but we're not kidnapping some corn-town local," Mrs. Santini said firmly. "I'll have to go speak to the parents."

Deirdre sagged. She'd come so very close, and now it was all over.

"You know what?" Rosie said. "I'll go meet her folks. Right now. You wanted to work on the act before tonight's show, didn't you? And I need to stretch my legs anyway."

Deirdre watched Mrs. Santini anxiously. She looked undecided. "I don't know. No, I really should be the one— What do you think, Tony?"

"Seems all right to me." Mr. Santini shrugged. "What's the difference if it's you or Rosie asking permission? No difference."

"I guess not, but—"

"We don't have much time."

"I know. I was thinking, if Carl paddles stage left and then runs all the way back around..." Mrs. Santini said.

"Well, let's try it now."

Mrs. Santini bit her lip and hesitated. She looked from her husband to Deirdre. "Rosie, tell them we'll watch out for her, keep her with our own kids," she finally said. "What's your name?"

"Deirdre O'Rourke."

"Do you want to do this, Deirdre?" Mrs. Santini asked. "For yourself?"

"Oh, yes!" Deirdre said. "Yes, I do!"

"Not because your mother's pushing you?"

"She's fourteen, she knows her own mind," Rosie said. "I'll change and we'll go."

"Make sure you get something in writing from the O'Rourkes," Mr. Santini said. "Signed by both of them, just in case."

Rosie nodded. "Will do."

Soon Deirdre and Rosie France were walking up Maple Street. Then they went around the long block of Sycamore Avenue three times.

"Me, a Santini! I'm so happy!" I'll be with Sean soon, she thought.

"The Santinis are okay," Rosie said. "They'll treat you fair."

Deirdre twirled a lock of hair around her finger. "But—what about the haircuts? I don't care, but—do I have to—?"

"What?"

"I heard that man yelling before, and Mr. Santini yelled back about haircuts."

"What? I don't know what you're talking about." Then Rosie broke into a big smile, and her dimples were deep, exactly the way they looked on stage; they were definitely real. "Oh, I know! 'The Santinis don't play to the haircuts.' See, the last spot's always the worst in a show, that's when they get the audience out of the theater. Playing to the haircuts, 'cause that's what you see when they're all going up the aisle."

"Oh. Oh, I get it." Vaudeville folks spoke a whole different language, Deirdre thought.

"Think I've been gone long enough? Figure five minutes to your house, ten, fifteen minutes with the parents, five minutes back," Rosie said. "Because I have to get my makeup on soon...Well, maybe once more around... Everyone thinks I'm nuts, I'm the only one takes it off between shows, but that greasepaint's murder on my skin."

"Thanks, Rosie! Gosh, I don't know how to thank you enough!"

"You're sure you told me the truth? I hope I'm not buying myself a load of trouble."

"The Gansworthys don't want me. I swear. They'll be happy I'm gone." And, Deirdre thought, I'll have to see them only one more time! She started to skip.

"Okay, then, I'll write the note. 'We give permission for our daughter...' It's a good thing you printed your name out for me, I better spell it right. Apostrophe after the O… So, you'll get your things and meet us at the station after the show. That train leaves at midnight. If you ain't there, it's taking off without you."

"Oh, I'll be there! Thanks, thanks, thanks!"

Deirdre already felt miles away from the Gansworthys and Miss Harrow and all of them. She was on her way to Texas and to Sean!

SEVENTEEN

"It's seven o'clock, miss!" Mrs. Gansworthy said. Her fork clanged against her dessert plate. "You can march straight to your room without any supper!"

"Now, Margaret..." Reverend Gansworthy said.

"She has to learn, doesn't she? Go on, up to your room!"

Deirdre glanced at the table. Blueberry pie. Oh, well. She went upstairs without a word.

Anyway, Deirdre thought, it was good that she didn't have to sit with them at the table tonight. Because she couldn't stop smiling.

The midnight train! The Gansworthys usually turned in around ten. If she waited to make sure they were asleep, that would be eleven. Plenty of time.

The aromas of chicken and pie crust drifted up to her room. Okay, she was hungry, but she didn't care—soon she'd be on her way!

She'd take nothing but the blue dress she had come with. No, wait, no sense in foolish pride. She needed clothes, and a coat for sure in this weather, and wouldn't they just go back into the used bin at church?

The laundry bag—that would work. It took all of five minutes to stuff her things together. Everything except Norma's old dress; she left that rattling on its wire hanger in the closet. There was one last thing she had to do—leave a note for the Gansworthys.

> Dear Reverend and Mrs. Gansworthy,
>   I've gone back to New York City to be
> with my mother. All I took was clothes. If you
> look, you'll see nothing else is missing.
>   Deirdre O'Rourke

They didn't want her, but she was steering them in the wrong direction anyway. Deirdre chewed on the pencil. Now that she was almost out the door, she could forgive the Gansworthys for not liking her. So she added:

> P.S. Thank you for taking me in and feeding me
> and all.

She propped the note up on the dresser. The room looked completely impersonal, as if she had never lived there. There was nothing left to do but watch the minute hand slowly turn around the clock.

She went to the window and looked for Rex. He was on his chain next to the Crowells' back steps. He was lying down, his head resting on his front paws; he looked so sweet and so lonely. She knew that he'd wait patiently for her in the afternoons; he'd wonder why she deserted him.

"I wish I could say I'll come to see you sometime," she whispered. Her breath left a mark on the cold window glass. She knew she would never be back this way again. "You're my only friend in Greenville. I love you, Rex."

She wished she could say good-bye and pet him one last time. But he'd give his excited bark when she approached. It was too risky—the Gansworthys might hear and maybe check.

Finally, she heard their footsteps on the stairs, water running in the bathroom sink, and then their bedroom door closing. Soon the house became quiet and dark. She made herself wait, just to be sure.

Deirdre picked up the laundry bag. This was the first big decision she'd made all by herself, she thought, without Sean's help. She hoped it was the right one.

At eleven-fifteen, she tiptoed out of the house and ran.

Deirdre arrived at the station too early, long before the midnight train or the showfolk. She waited off to the side, shivering in the dark cold under the big trees. The platform looked empty in the moonlight, but she couldn't take a chance on someone spotting her. She didn't dare come out of the shadows until the vaudeville troupe appeared.

Finally, they came in a big noisy group. They were talking too loudly; she was afraid they'd attract attention. When she spotted the red hair shining under the station lights, Deirdre ran over.

"Hi, Rosie! I'm here! I made it!"

"Oh. That's good."

Deirdre followed alongside Rosie—she wanted to be with her on the train—but Rosie said, "You'd better stay with the Santinis."

"But I thought—I thought we'd sit together and—and we'd talk and—"

"Look, kid, I was glad to help you out, no skin off my nose," Rosie said, "but don't expect me to take care of you, okay? Anyway, the Santinis need to break you into the act before we hit Topeka."

Deirdre stepped back, awkward and hurt. She didn't need anyone to take care of her!

Now Deirdre was sitting up straight next to Mr. Santini on the idling train. Why didn't it go? She was tense and alert. As long as the train was in Greenville, something could go wrong, somebody could stop her at the last minute. What if the Gansworthys woke up and found her note and came swooping down the platform? Why was it taking so long?

Then the whistle blew and the engine began to chug. Slowly the train eased out of the station. It picked up speed as it passed the corner of Main Street. And Deirdre was home free!

It was dark outside, but she thought she saw the Mackinsaw Bridge, way outside of Greenville, whizzing by.

Her body went limp with relief. The train was too warm. That, and the lateness of the hour, made waves of sleepiness crash over her. She fought to keep her eyes open.

Deirdre was surrounded by strangers, on another train barreling through the night, rushing to the unknown, and this time, Sean wasn't next to her. Like when she awoke in panic and his seat was empty…This isn't the orphan train, Deirdre comforted herself, this is vaudeville. But she was an outsider.

Rosie was the only one she knew. Her red hair was like a beacon in the middle of the car. She was sitting next to a lady—the poodle lady?—and leaning across the aisle to talk to one of the Ping Brothers. Deirdre could hear her laughing. Rosie had helped her, Deirdre thought, and she couldn't blame Rosie if she had other friends to sit with. But Deirdre had felt such a strong connection even before they met, way back when Rosie was on stage at the Victoria and seemed to be singing "When Irish Eyes Are Smiling" directly to her.

Deirdre looked around in sleepy confusion. All the others were ghost images, faces she'd seen from a distance. Charlie Morgan—he was lots older in person. He was playing cards with another Ping Brother, the unicycle boy, and the Great Regurgitator. Others were clustered together, talking and joking. She felt so alone. She thought she heard Marie, the youngest Santini, telling her, "The Pings don't get along…except on stage…" but maybe she was dreaming. Everything had happened so fast, it all felt like a dream. There was the poodle lady, surrounded by dog cases and…

Deirdre nodded off. Mr. Santini's hand on her shoulder brought her back.

"Can you read music?" he asked.

"I don't know." She was embarrassed; she didn't know what "reading" music meant.

Mr. Santini sighed and handed Deirdre the sheet music anyway. "All right, follow the words, and I'll sing the melody. Listen. 'Take me back to old Napoli, where my *mamma mia* waits for me, with *pasta fazool* by the bright blue sea, oh, how I miss old Napoli.'"

On "sea," Mr. Santini had to hit a high note, and he couldn't make it.

"All right, now you," Mr. Santini said.

She sang, following the words on the sheet. Her voice felt leaden, everything heavy with sleepiness.

"No, listen. 'With *pasta fazoo-ool...*'" Mr. Santini said. "Try it again."

Deirdre repeated the song as best she could.

"Not bad. Now put the words down and see if you can—"

"Look at her, Tony, she's dead on her feet," Mrs. Santini interrupted. "Save it for morning."

"She's got three more verses to memorize before Topeka."

"They're not hard to—"

Deirdre didn't hear the rest of it.

Someone was shaking her arm. Deirdre didn't know where she was, and then she heard Mrs. Santini's voice.

"Sorry, hon, time to wake up."

It seemed as if only a minute had gone by, but when Deirdre looked out the window, it was hazy light and they were coming into a station.

"Aw, Ma..." Marie mumbled.

"Let's go, kids," Mrs. Santini continued. "Vincent, get the big suitcase, and Carl, you grab the little one."

"It's five o'clock in the morning," the younger Santini son complained.

The train stopped, and everyone was getting off, carrying all kinds of baggage. Deirdre read the sign: TOPEKA. Her mouth felt like cotton.

The Great Regurgitator was arguing with the stationmaster. "What do you mean, no cabs? What kind of town is this, anyway?"

"Decent folk are home in their beds at this hour," the stationmaster sneered.

The stationmaster wasn't home in his bed, either, Deirdre thought. He was like Mrs. Gansworthy; he thought they were a bunch of ragtag gypsies.

Trixie Dee sighed. "So we'll walk to the theater. Good thing it's downtown."

"Outrageous!" That was Charlie Morgan. "I'll have a word with Bremer about this!"

"What? You think you're still on the Keith circuit?" Trixie said.

Someone gave Deirdre one of the dog cases to carry. It was heavy, though the poodle in it was small. Rosie smiled at her, so Deirdre struggled to catch up. Topeka was much bigger than Greenville. They walked for blocks and blocks through empty streets.

"That one's Gigi," Rosie said. "She's my favorite."

"I used to have a dog named Rex," Deirdre said.

The poodle was quiet; she seemed used to being caged and carried. But behind them, Charlie Morgan kept roaring, "Outrageous!"

"Charlie still expects star treatment. He never traveled with Allstate Variety before, that's for sure," Rosie said. "Until South Bend, he was taking a Pullman. La-di-da. Until he drank up his dough."

"But he is a star," Deirdre said.

"Yeah, he still gets next-to-last spot. I think I should."

"I think so, too," Deirdre said loyally. So, next-to-last was the best. The Six Santinis were someplace in the middle; she couldn't remember where.

"He played the Palace ages ago. Same bill as Eddie Cantor. And he doesn't let anybody forget it."

Deirdre tried not to drag her feet. The dog seemed to be getting heavier. The laundry bag in her other hand wasn't light, either.

"I have no patience with someone who throws it all away," Rosie continued. "Well, he pulls himself together for his act, I'll say that much for him." She rolled her shoulders. "I hate sleeping on the train. It leaves me stiff as a board."

"I was supposed to learn the Napoli song, but I fell

asleep," Deirdre said. "The Santinis don't have accents. Why do they—?"

"The Santinis work the Italian dialect, Maxie and Shane do the Yiddish, I throw a bit of brogue into 'Rosie O'Grady.'"

Maxie and Shane—they were the comic team. "But why?" Deirdre asked.

Rosie shrugged. "It gets laughs from the rubes."

"The rubes?"

"The civilians." Rosie saw Deirdre's puzzled look and added, "The audience."

Do they all think I'm a rube? Deirdre wondered. Only yesterday, she was poor-little-orphan-train-girl. So much had happened so fast; she didn't know what she was now.

The sun was just coming up as they reached the theater. The Grand looked lots fancier than the Victoria. No one was there yet to let them in.

Trixie Dee was red-faced and panting. She dropped her suitcase with a thump. They waited in front of the stage door with their luggage piled on the sidewalk. In the faint sunlight, they looked like any group of people, all sizes and shapes, with fatigue all over their faces. On second glance, though, there was something proud about the way they held themselves, some hidden magic, Deirdre thought.

The poodle lady let the poodles out of their cases. Show business is hard, Deirdre thought, even for dogs.

Vincent Santini and the unicycle boy went down the street to get coffee and doughnuts for everyone.

"Why couldn't we go to the rooming house first and get some shut-eye?" Carl Santini whined to his mother.

"Why couldn't we?" Deirdre whispered to Rosie.

"Because if you check in at five in the morning, they charge you for the whole night," Rosie said. "This way we get a chance to rehearse first—we hardly ever do—and anyway, there'll be cabs around later; the rooming house is on the other side of town."

Topeka was waking up. Some people appeared on the street, early birds on the way to work. The Gansworthys might be just waking up. It would be a while before they read her note. She was still safe.

Deirdre was devouring a sugar doughnut when Mr. Santini came over to her.

"All right, Deirdre," he said, "the second verse. 'Take me back to old Napoli, where the *paisanos* call to me, I gotta find a way across the sea…'"

She swallowed the last of the doughnut, cleared her throat, and tried to sing along. The tune was easy enough, except for that high note on "sea," but there were so many words to memorize! However hard show business might be, it had to be better than Miss Harrow's class. That was behind her now. She didn't know what lay ahead—but each train ride would bring her that much closer to Texas.

EIGHTEEN

It was the Great Regurgitator's turn on stage. He needed only a few drumrolls, so some of the musicians tipped back in their chairs with their hats over their eyes, and the pianist was chomping a sandwich.

There was a lot of waiting around, Deirdre thought.

"We're lucky to get the stage for a run-through," Mr. Santini told Deirdre. "We won't have another chance, so pay attention." They were sitting in the third row. "During the show, when the Regurgitator's on, we have to be ready in the wings."

She hated to ask him another dumb question. She was glad when he added, on his own, "Wings. The sides of the stage, behind the curtains."

"Okay."

"You know the words now?"

"Pretty well."

"Because there's word cues for our moves. You understand? You can't get the verses mixed up." Deirdre could tell he was nervous about her; that made her nervous, too.

In the back of the auditorium, the Ping Brothers were throwing clubs back and forth. On the side, Rosie was practicing her curtsy—sometimes dipping lower, sometimes sweeping her arms wider. Charlie Morgan threw his straw hat in the air, caught it on his cane, and flipped it back on to his head, just the way she'd seen in the show. He did it over and over again. Deirdre was surprised to see them working on things that they must have done a million times already.

The Regurgitator finished, and Deirdre followed the Santinis toward the stage.

"What's your name again?" the piano player asked her as she went by.

"Deirdre O'Rourke."

"Deirdre, what key do you need?"

"Key?"

He rolled his eyes and sighed. "Just sing a couple of lines… Okay, good enough."

"Deirdre, enter stage left and go straight downstage, far as you can get, leave us plenty of room," Mr. Santini told her.

Deirdre looked frantically in one direction and another.

"She's got that look again!" Marie piped up.

"Don't be afraid to ask if you don't understand," Mrs. Santini said. "Downstage is toward the footlights; upstage is behind you, going toward the back wall."

"When you face the audience, your left hand is stage left and your right hand is stage right," Marie said. "It's easy!"

Even an eight-year-old knew more than she did!

Deirdre got into position. The Santinis were someplace behind her. She didn't know what to do with her arms. She had an audience of *showfolk!* Her mouth felt dry.

There were four chords from the piano—and then a silence. Should she have started?

"Let's go, Deirdre, what're you waiting for?" Mr. Santini's voice came from behind her. She shrank with embarrassment.

Mr. Santini sighed. "From the top, Mike."

The chords again, and she made herself plunge into the song. There was none of that free and easy feeling. She wasn't singing well, she knew it; she was concentrating too hard on remembering the words. Her eyes darted around the auditorium. She was glad the other showpeople were hardly watching; everyone seemed busy with something.

"...with *pasta fazoo-ool* by the bright blue sea..." She barely managed to make the high note. There were loud thumps behind her. She caught a glimpse of Marie's somersaults, one rolling into the next, and so fast! How did she do that!

"...where the *paisanos* call to me, I gotta find a way across the sea..." Out of the corner of her eye, she saw Carl jumping up on Vincent's shoulders and rowing like mad. Whew, she got through all the verses without stumbling.

"Good," Mr. Santini said. "That was okay. But don't look at what we're doing. Keep your attention out front. The whole time."

"Okay."

"You think she's ready for the matinee?" he asked Mrs. Santini.

"Sure, let her get her feet wet," Mrs. Santini answered.

Deirdre bit her lips. She didn't know anything about the stage, and next time she'd have to do it for real!

"It's better with all of us tumbling, isn't it, Pa?" Marie asked.

"Yes, much better."

"We'll get the laughs now, won't we, Pa?" Marie said. "I don't ever want Tina's part again!"

At the rooming house, Deirdre tried on Tina's costume. It was red-and-green satin, and miles too big and long. Tina must be so busty! Deirdre thought. Mrs. Santini pinned and tucked for the longest time.

Through the pins in her mouth, Mrs. Santini said, "You're a good girl, Deirdre. A quick study, too. And you're standing nice and still for me—I know that's hard."

Deirdre flushed with pleasure.

She and Marie had to take a nap before the show. They were going to share a bed for the whole tour; that was okay, Deirdre was used to sharing and Marie was very small. Mrs. Santini tucked them in, just like a real mother. Of course, Marie was her daughter, but Mrs. Santini tucked Deirdre in, too, and with a soft stroke on her cheek. She almost wanted to arch up and rub her cheek against Mrs. Santini's hand like a cat.

Marie chattered at her for a while—she was like a pesty kid sister, too talkative and giggly, but cute. Marie fell asleep soon. Deirdre closed her eyes, but worry kept her awake. "Take me back to old Napoli..." It wasn't a good song, she thought, and some of the words made no sense to her. *Pasta fazool. Paisanos.* She went over the verses in her mind. Sense or not, she had them memorized.

Soon it was time to go back to the Grand. Backstage was a little nicer than at the Victoria—it was warm—but it was still just one big dressing room with one long mirror for everybody. Mrs. Santini sat Deirdre in front of the mirror and told her to watch while she put greasepaint on Deirdre's face. "Pay attention so you can learn to do it yourself," she said.

Deirdre's face turned orangy, and then there was rouge and lipstick, too! Mrs. Santini put red dots in the inside corners of Deirdre's eyes and blended white triangles at the outside corners. She beaded Deirdre's eyelashes with black mascara. Deirdre stared at herself in the mirror—she looked like a painted lady, even worse than Big Polly's ladies back on Division Street!

Deirdre whispered, "I look like a—like a—"

"Trust me, hon," Mrs. Santini said. "The lights wash everything out. Without makeup, you'd be a ghost. A ghost with no eyes."

Deirdre could just imagine what Mrs. Gansworthy would say!

"Listen to me, Deirdre. It's all right. Look, look at Rosie over there, and Gloria."

146

It was true. Rosie was painted up the same way, and she was leaning toward the mirror to glue on fake eyelashes! She'd looked perfectly beautiful on stage at the Victoria, hadn't she? And Gloria, the poodle lady, was sponging rouge on her cheeks.

Deirdre took a deep breath. She had to decide right here and now to trust Mrs. Santini. Vaudeville was a different world, and she was in it now.

Mrs. Santini laughed. "It's just for the stage. You know, nothing in the Bible says makeup is a sin."

Mrs. Santini had sewn up Tina's costume. Deirdre hid behind a screen and quickly slipped it on. It almost fit. Gloria came by; she tied the sash tighter around Deirdre's waist and said, "There, now that's good!"

"Five minutes!" someone called.

Trixie Dee hugged everyone. Deirdre, too. "She needs to do that before every show," Vincent explained. "For good luck."

"Break a leg, kid," Maxie said to her. What an awful thing to say to somebody! But he had a warm smile.

"Five minutes!" And suddenly time was zooming by, double-time, minutes turning into seconds, and the Great Regurgitator was putting out the fire with a stream of water and Deirdre was in the wings stage left with Marie and Mr. Santini, and Mrs. Santini, Carl, and Vincent were stage right, ready to run on, and out in the dark, there were people, so many people; she could hardly see them, she could hear them, breathing and rustling and clapping. This wasn't like singing in the street, it wasn't anything like it, why hadn't she thought of that? Wait, hold everything, she wasn't ready for this!

"Go." Mr. Santini pushed her on. The spotlight was blinding. Four chords and she started the song. She kept her attention out front like she was supposed to, but the thumps behind her were much louder than in rehearsal, and the Santinis were yelling out in broken English, and then the audience was laughing! The first laughs startled her, and she almost stumbled on the words, but she kept on going and got used to that audience roar, sort of, but she was distracted and shaky. And then they all took their bows, fast, fast, running, the way Mr. Santini wanted, and there was applause, they ran off, and it was over. She knew she hadn't done well.

She ran past Rosie in the wings. Rosie didn't even glance at Deirdre. She seemed to be somewhere else, and she was stretching her leg up high against the wall, so high her underpants showed and everyone could see, Carl, Vincent, and everyone...

"Ladies and gentlemen, for your entertainment and delectation, presenting the international star—ROSIE FRANCE!"

Backstage, Deirdre could hear Rosie's music swelling up with the first line of "The Daughter of Rosie O'Grady."

"Great." Mr. Santini hugged Deirdre. "Good job." She was surprised and relieved; she thought he'd be disappointed in her.

"Did you hear them?" Carl said. "We killed 'em!"

"We slayed 'em!" Vincent said.

Deirdre was shivery and hot all at once. The Santinis were happy, so maybe she wasn't that terrible. But she hadn't done her best. Nowhere near her best. The Santinis didn't seem to mind, she did get through all the verses, and after all, it was her first time. And the applause at the end… She wanted another chance at it. She couldn't wait for another chance at it!

She heard Rosie belting out "When Irish Eyes Are Smiling."

Next time she'd know to expect the loud thumps and yelling behind her, Deirdre thought; next time, she wouldn't be startled. She wouldn't lose her concentration. Next time—tonight!

"You ain't seen nothin' yet!" Rosie called out.

You ain't seen nothin' yet, Deirdre whispered to herself.

All they ate between shows was some orange sections. For energy, Mrs. Santini said. Deirdre was too excited to be hungry, and the Santinis couldn't do their act on full stomachs.

"We go to a diner after the last show," Marie told her, "and I get apple pie!"

Rosie creamed her greasepaint off, but no one else did.

"Don't bother," Mrs. Santini said. "There's not that much time."

"Getting it off is the worst," Marie put in. "That hurts!"

"No, it doesn't," Mrs. Santini said. "Don't tell Deirdre that. It's a nuisance, that's all."

"It does, too! When you rub too hard. And when I get cold cream in my eyes!"

They hung around backstage. There was nothing to do at the rooming house, and anyway, it was a cab ride away. Some of the people wandered out for a snack. Gloria took the poodles for their run. The Ping Brothers scattered in different directions. One of them stayed to play cards with the Regurgitator, the unicycle boy, and Maxie of Maxie and Shane. She could see they were playing for money—that was *gambling,* Deirdre thought; Reverend Gansworthy had given a sermon about it.

At the rooming house, she was registered under the Santinis' name. Even if the Gansworthys knew where to look, Deirdre thought, they wouldn't find a trace of her. Not that the Gansworthys cared about her, but she'd bet anything they'd reported her to the police. What did the police do to runaways? She'd feel safer when Kansas was far behind her. After tonight's show, one more day in Topeka, and they'd travel on…

Tonight's show. Waiting made Deirdre restless. She went to sit with Rosie. Rosie had seemed so friendly on the walk over to the theater, almost like a big sister. She was the person to ask: Had her performance not been as bad as she'd thought? Was she too hard on herself? Or were the Santinis just being kind?

Rosie was talking to the trumpet player, but finally she turned to Deirdre. "Well, how did it go?"

"All right, I guess. Mr. Santini said I did a good job,"

Deirdre answered. "Didn't you see?"

"I don't see anything when I'm preparing to go on." She stretched. "I kind of turn inward."

"Oh." Deirdre covered her disappointment. It made sense to shut everything out just before you went on, she thought. She'd try to do that tonight.

The six musicians mostly kept to themselves, but the trumpet player stayed around Rosie, so Deirdre couldn't talk to her that much. That was okay; Deirdre needed time to think about her song.

No matter how she looked at it, the lyrics weren't very good. In fact, bad. "Take me back to old Napoli." She had to find a way to put some feeling into it. Maybe…if she forgot about "old Napoli" and *"pasta fazool"*—Carl told her that was some kind of macaroni and beans, what a dumb thing to put to music! But if she forgot about that, the song was about wanting very badly to go somewhere. The way she was longing to get to Texas. "I gotta find a way across the sea…" Ready to do anything to get there, run away with a vaudeville troupe even, *anything*. "Oh, how I miss old Napoli…" Oh, how she missed Sean! If she could think of that while she was singing, she could do it right, she knew she could! But if she got distracted, it would fall as flat as it did this afternoon. Even worse. Maybe it was too hard to think about other things and remember lyrics she'd just learned. If she mixed up the words, the Santinis' antics would get all mixed up, too! She was excited, and she was scared. She didn't know.

Finally, the call. "Five minutes!" The Ping Brothers. Trixie Dee and "Hannah does the hula-ha, hula-ha, hula-ha…" The Great Regurgitator. Waiting in the wings. "It's a full house," someone whispered. Then: "The comedy toast-a of New York-a! The SIX SANTINIS!"

NINETEEN

The four chords, and Deirdre's heart was hammering. She plunged into the first line. "Take me back to old Napoli…" The spotlight still blinded her, but that was okay, it felt warm and…No time to think of the exact things she'd planned, the music kept going and the words came on top of each other too fast. But she held on to the feeling, to the longing inside, and she shut out the antics behind her.

"Where my *mamma mia* waits for me…"

She sang out her loneliness and despair, and letting it go felt so right, her voice was strong and true…She was prepared for the audience's laughs this time, they didn't seem so very loud now.

"I gotta find a way across the sea…"

She hit the high note, hit it easy on a wave of emotion. That's where Carl would be leaping up and paddling like mad, but there were only a few guffaws. The people in the dark were listening to her, she could feel it! They were going beyond the dumb words with her, down deep to all the mixed-up things in her heart...

"Come-a on in the boat-a," Vincent yelled out behind her, but then another voice, a voice from the audience called, "Let the girl sing!"

The Santinis sounded ever more frantic, but out front there was a hush and "Hey, give the girl a chance!"

Something warm and wonderful was coming at Deirdre across the footlights. They were with her all the way!

Deirdre broke the mood for the last two lines. She couldn't keep a big smile from spreading and spreading. She didn't need to see them; she could feel them leaning forward and smiling back at her. She was bathed in a golden glow.

It was over too soon. Then the bows, quick, quick, the way Mr. Santini wanted, and oh, all that applause! She wasn't nothing; they loved her, and she wished she could go on and on. She was the cat's pajamas, she was the top of the top!

Deirdre ran into the wings, breathless and tingling. Rosie circled her thumb and finger in the A-okay sign. Then a voice boomed, "...international star—ROSIE FRANCE!" and Rosie twirled on stage in a flurry of ruffles. "I'm the daughter of Rosie O'Grady."

The music, everything, it was all so exciting! And Rosie had watched her act and thought she was A-okay! Deirdre turned to the Santinis, wide open for their praise. This time, she'd been really good! But Mrs. Santini frowned and Mr. Santini's face was grim. Confused, Deirdre followed them backstage.

Mr. Santini's voice was icy. "Lesson one. You never upstage your own act!"

Deirdre was too shocked to speak.

"But—but—I stayed downstage the whole time," she finally stammered.

Mr. Santini turned away from her.

"Thanks a whole lot, kid," Vincent said with a cutting look.

The Santinis rushed down the corridor into the dressing room. Deirdre hesitated in the doorway; she stood alone, awkward and miserable. It had felt so right, how could she be wrong about that? But even Marie looked mad!

"I haven't seen anything quite like that in a long time." Charlie Morgan was suddenly next to Deirdre. "Certainly not on this circuit."

What did that mean? Nothing here made any sense at all!

"You had them in the palm of your hand," he continued. "They loved you."

"But the Santinis are mad at me," Deirdre whispered. "I don't understand."

"You don't know, do you?" Charlie Morgan shook his head. "Poor child, you're the straight man."

"I don't understand. I didn't miss any words, not one. I

did my very best and I wasn't upstage, I stayed where I was supposed to, but Mr. Santini said—"

"Ah, my dear. When an actor moves too far upstage, that forces his co-actors to look at him and turn their backs to the audience. You see? So it's come to mean any way of drawing attention to yourself and sabotaging the others." He chuckled. "Watch what Maxie does to Shane sometimes, all sorts of shtick on Shane's best lines."

"But—all I did was sing the song."

"Far too well. The Six Santinis is comedy. Tina Santini had a scratchy little voice and never could hit that high C. Quite perfect."

"Oh." Deirdre swallowed hard. "Oh. No one told me."

"I suppose they didn't think they had to. Who'd expect star quality to come out of nowhere?" He laughed and shook his head. "Out of Greenville, Kansas, no less."

Star quality? Charlie Morgan was talking about her!

"Deirdre?" Mrs. Santini called. "Come along and get your makeup off."

Deirdre walked stiff-legged to the end of the long makeup table where the Santinis were gathered. They hated her now. What if they fired her—then what would she do?

Mrs. Santini sat Deirdre down and handed over a jar of cold cream. "Put lots on," she said. "You have to get every bit of greasepaint out of your pores. You can tissue it off by yourself, can't you?"

"Yes," Deirdre said. She was afraid to look at anyone.

She concentrated on removing the orange glop.

"Deirdre," Mrs. Santini said, "I understand. Mr. Santini has a temper, but he'll come around. We know this is all new to you. You're just a child, and you didn't mean any harm."

"I didn't," Deirdre whispered. It was so unfair!

"You have to downplay the song. Don't sing all out for the next show, just get the words out and that's it. The way you did the first time was fine. Can you do that?"

Deirdre met her eyes. "The next show?"

Mrs. Santini nodded. "Hon, we all like you, and we'll give you another chance, okay? If you can remember—it's our routine that counts." She shrugged. "I mean, that's the act."

"I'll remember, I promise." Deirdre was so relieved that she could stay. She couldn't get to Texas by herself. And she wanted to be on that stage again! Well—at least until she found Sean.

It took a lot of cream and a lot of tissues to work the makeup off. Marie didn't have to do it all by herself; Mrs. Santini was busy helping her. Okay, Marie was only eight, but Deirdre couldn't help wishing…Anyway, Mrs. Santini did like her, she'd said so.

"Not so hard, that hurts," Marie complained.

Deirdre leaned toward the mirror as she wiped off the last traces of mascara. "Mr. Morgan's a star, isn't he?"

"Charlie? He played the Palace once—you should've seen him in those days!—but his weakness for the bottle killed it," Mrs. Santini said. "It's a shame."

The ladies in Greenville had said Charlie Morgan could light up a stage. Even Mrs. Gansworthy had agreed. He was the best one in the show—he had the next-to-last spot, didn't he? So Charlie Morgan *knew* about star quality. No matter what, Deirdre had his words to hug close.

TWENTY

There were two more shows in Topeka. Deirdre tried, but she couldn't sing the song as shakily as she had that very first, scared time. Something sneaked through, something that reached out to the audience.

At least they didn't yell, "Let the girl sing." But the Santinis weren't getting the big laughs, and Mr. Santini was worried.

On the train to Fort Collins, he said, "Don't take the words so seriously, Deirdre. It's *supposed* to be a stupid song. Listen, don't hit that high note anymore—give us a screech."

Two days in Fort Collins, three shows a day. And Deirdre screeched. On stage, she was in misery. Now she knew she had the power to hold an audience, and it was terrible to pretend she didn't. And the Santinis still weren't getting enough laughs. It didn't matter, she kept telling herself, she was going to peel off in Texas anyway.

Two a day in Walton Falls. There was a storm that

night, and the windows of the rooming house rattled. Lightning flashed through the dark, and thunder crashed into Deirdre's dreams. She dreamed thunderous knocking on the door, and it meant danger; maybe if she didn't sing too well, they'd leave her alone. She didn't make the high note—she didn't!—but two huge policemen broke the door down anyway and grabbed her arms. "Please don't take me back to the Gansworthys," she begged. They tied her up and laughed. "The Gansworthys don't want a sow's ear." They dragged her across the floor like a roped calf. "You're going straight to the orphanage for runaways." She struggled and screamed for Rosie. Rosie shrugged: "Sorry, no skin off my nose." Deirdre fought and scratched and cried for help, and no one came…

She woke up imprisoned in the twisted sheets. Marie was asleep beside her. Deirdre listened to Marie's peaceful breathing, and slowly her heart stopped thumping. Nothing but a nightmare, she told herself. But she stared into the dark, scared and alone. She needed to be with her brother.

The next morning, Deirdre wrote to Sean. She wrote about how awful the Gansworthys and Greenville had been. She told him the exact dates and theaters they'd play in Fort Worth, Houston, and Galveston so he could hitch to whichever was closest to Bandera. He could meet her backstage, and then they'd figure out where to go. Soon, she thought, soon! "Tear up this letter and don't tell where I am," she warned, "because the Gansworthys might report me." She wrote about the show, too, but she didn't tell him about her part. She was too ashamed of her fake singing.

Two a day in another town, a rooming house with bedbugs, and on to Cranston. Frozen fields and occasional clusters of houses speeded by Deirdre's train window. The yellow dots of dandelions and puffballs she'd seen along other tracks were long gone now. Sometimes other passengers gave the boisterous vaudeville troupe dirty looks, but no one cared. Steel wheels sparked against the tracks and rolled Deirdre farther and farther from the Gansworthys.

They had to work on Christmas Eve and Christmas Day. But after, there was a party in Maxie and Shane's room. The unicycle boy brought marzipan. Gloria sang "I Wish I Could Shimmy Like My Sister Kate." Rosie showed Deirdre the shimmy, and they did it together, shaking and wiggling, and everyone clapped. Deirdre could just imagine Mrs. Gansworthy's shocked, pinched face! Later, they all sang "Silent Night," Deirdre harmonizing, and Gene, the trumpet player, wove the melody around and between the voices and let it drift into the starry night outside. It was beautiful. It was a good Christmas.

Deirdre wondered if the same starry sky was shining over Sean. She wondered if Jimmy or Mum was remembering her tonight. Christmases at home hadn't been that merry. The city sparkled with lights, the stores displayed rich, wonderful things, restaurants filled with festive crowds—and none of it for poor people. A charity Christmas dinner tasted worse than no dinner at all.

The troupe moved on. Sometimes they had to catch a train right after the last show and ride through the night. Deirdre curled up in her seat and got used to sleeping through the *bump-bump-bump* of the wheels. The scenery outside the train window was changing. They were leaving flat farmland behind. There were hills and valleys and blue-gray mountains in the distance.

In Hillsdale, Rosie twisted her ankle just before the first matinee and it was swelling up bad. Backstage, she wrapped wet rags around it and grimaced with pain. But on cue, she swirled on stage with the same sparkling smile. Deirdre, watching from the wings, was amazed to see her dance the cancan with every one of the high kicks; if she was favoring her ankle, you sure couldn't tell. Though after every show in Hillsdale, Rosie came off stage pale and gritting her teeth.

"How does she do it?" Deirdre asked Marie.

"Last year I went on with the measles," Marie said. "We covered the spots with makeup, and after the act, Pa wrapped me up in a blanket and carried me to the rooming house."

There are no days off in vaudeville, Deirdre thought.

On the trains, Mrs. Santini drilled Marie and Carl on the multiplication tables. She told Deirdre to pay attention, too, but Deirdre was restless. She liked to sit with Rosie whenever she could, or talk to the other showfolk. She learned things from them that were lots more interesting than five times five.

"Never whistle in the dressing room."

"The first spot's always a silent one, something easy to ignore, because the people are still coming in." Oh, so that's why the Pings were glum—and they worked so hard, too! Lou Ping was the friendly one. Between Walton Falls and Highmount, he taught her how to juggle four oranges.

Mr. Morgan called the stage "the boards."

A gimmick was insurance, Maxie told her. It was your own bit of business, your signature shtick, your ace in the hole; if nothing else was working with the audience, you had your gimmick to count on. And he showed her his special double takes and triple takes. Deirdre laughed and laughed—he was so funny!

But then she overheard Shane fighting with Maxie. "Cut it out! Stop chewing the scenery!" And Deirdre had to admit that though Maxie was funny and nice, he was a real hambone.

"Trumpet players are the best kissers," Rosie told her. "On account of the calluses on their lips." Deirdre was proud that Rosie confided in her—until she heard Rosie say the exact same thing to Gloria and later to Trixie. Anyway, Rosie was treating her like a grownup.

Mr. Morgan taught her to tap the Shuffle-off-to-Buffalo steps. When she got the hang of it, he put his straw hat on her head, hooked his arm through hers, and up and down the rooming-house halls, they shuffled off like nobody's business!

In a diner, Trixie Dee sneaked a ketchup packet into her

pocket. She nudged Deirdre to take one, too. Back in Trixie's room, they mixed them with water. "Vaudeville tomato juice," Trixie said. "Nutritious and free!" They clinked glasses and yelled, "Cheers!"

A baby-pink spotlight, a pink gel, was the best—it made you look your prettiest. Rosie insisted on that in every theater they came to.

Three shows a day in Highmount, makeup on, makeup off, another rooming house, another train—towns and theaters blurred in Deirdre's mind. All for those ten minutes on the boards. Each time, Deirdre was caught up in the excitement, and each time, holding back was agony. She wanted that golden glow again. She ached with wanting it.

"This isn't working," Mr. Santini said. "We're not getting the laughs we should, so I had someone watch from the front. You know what it is? You look miserable, Deirdre. No one wants to laugh if they're sorry for you. So could you please drop the tragedy?"

Two a day in Livingston. Deirdre tried to look happier. But she was singing about missing Napoli. Was she supposed to grin? She tried a smile; it felt frozen.

"That screech is going to destroy your voice," Rosie told her. "Don't push it from your vocal cords. Take a deep breath and fake it."

Rosie was like a big sister, at least some of the time. Rosie knew her secret, and she hadn't told anyone.

"What about 'the show must go on'?" Deirdre asked her. She had been worrying about that. "Is it terrible to run off? Is everyone going to think bad of me?" She cared too much about them now.

"If you were a headliner, I guess it would be pretty bad," Rosie said. "But what you do isn't... I mean, Marie can take over until the Santinis replace you. Anybody could fill in."

That was good, Deirdre thought, so why did it make her feel so bad? Because they had loved her in Topeka. She could do something special, something magical, if she had the chance.

"Should I tell the Santinis? Ahead of time? Mrs. Santini's so nice to me and—"

"You got to look out for yourself." Rosie frowned. "They couldn't just let you run away, you know. They think they're responsible for you—to your parents, remember?"

Deirdre bit her lip. Soon Colorado and then Texas. They were coming closer.

On the train to Wetherford, Deirdre spotted an empty seat next to Rosie and she dashed over. But Rosie put her hand in the way and winked. "Sorry, it's taken." And then Deirdre saw Gene, the trumpet player, heading toward Rosie.

Deirdre could understand that Rosie had romance on her mind, but she was hurt anyway. She stood helplessly rooted in the aisle.

"Come, sit with Grandpa." Mr. Morgan, across the aisle, patted the seat beside him, and Deirdre gratefully sank into it. She'd never had a grandpa. Or a grandma. It had been Mum, Sean, and Jimmy, and no one else.

Mr. Morgan would be a good grandpa, Deirdre thought. He was never a mean drunk or a fighting drunk, like some of the men at Gallagher's. He took steady nips from his silver flask, but they made him mellow. He covered the alcohol smell with peppermint, as if everyone didn't know and really believed it was cough medicine. He hardly ever stumbled on stage.

"Delighted to have your charming company on this journey," he said. Deirdre could tell he'd been drinking by how very careful he was not to slur his words; his speech was extra-crisp. "Don't mind too much about Rosie."

"Oh, I don't, I understand," Deirdre said quickly. "No one wants a little sister in the way when—"

"Dear child, don't expect to find a sister in her. You mustn't count on—"

"She helped me," Deirdre said. "You don't know how much she's helped me and—"

"And why not? Rosie has a good heart. Sure, she'll give you a hand if her own interests aren't at stake. But if they are, our Rosie, under all those dimples and smiles, is tough as they come. Yes, when all the rest are dinosaurs, I'll put my money on Rosie France clawing her way into the talking pictures."

Dinosaurs? He must have been drinking, Deirdre thought. "Well, Rosie's so talented and—"

"Not much of a singer and not much of a dancer, but she can certainly hold a stage, I'll give you that. All sparkle and personality, and legs to there."

"She's wonderful!"

"Don't get me wrong, I like her—though I know she's angling for my spot in the show."

So that's why he's saying bad things about her, Deirdre thought.

"Yes, Rosie France will survive," Mr. Morgan continued.

"Survive *what*?" He wasn't making any sense at all, and Deirdre was getting impatient with the conversation.

"Vaudeville. Vaudeville is on its deathbed, my dear. Look around you." He waved his arm extravagantly, taking in everyone in the car. "Dinosaurs, all of us. Vaudeville is on its last legs."

"No, it's not," Deirdre said.

"The talkies will kill it. Mark my words. *The Jazz Singer* is just the beginning."

"I saw that," Deirdre said. "But—"

"Who'll go to see a vaudeville show when they can get Al Jolson anytime and cheaper? All the theaters will show talking pictures, all the theaters in all the towns will tear out the footlights."

"But talkies aren't in person!"

"No lights, no bands, no temperaments, no problems. Trixie Dee, the Santinis, the Ping Brothers, the Great Regurgitator, Gloria and her poodles, and yes, Charlie Morgan—all dinosaurs. It's a dying art, my girl."

"It can't be!" Deirdre thought it was only the liquor talking, but he sounded so sure. His sadness was catching.

"What would happen to everyone? The Santinis?"

"They could go back to the circus, perhaps. They were circus people, did you know that? Aerialists. Mrs. Santini fell. No harm done, there was a safety net, but she lost her nerve and she didn't want the children in a high-wire act anymore. Circus—that's where their tumbling and acrobatics come from. Too bad they have to use the dialect."

"Why do they?" Sometimes it made Deirdre uncomfortable; it seemed as if the Santinis were mocking their own people.

"It makes the rubes laugh. Immigrants, different ways, languages they can't understand. Give them stereotypes to laugh at, and they feel less threatened... Now, what were we saying?... Ah, what will happen to everyone. I hope the unicycle boy can go home and learn a trade..."

Vaudeville is too wonderful to die, Deirdre thought. She loved the way they banded together as they traveled from town to town. She loved that hushed moment before they faced a new audience. She loved everything about it. He had to be wrong!

"Don't be sad, my dear." The flask went to Mr. Morgan's mouth. "There'll be a place for you somewhere, Miss Deirdre O'Rourke. You have a shining talent that can't be denied forever. You could be a great star."

"Do you think so, Mr. Morgan?"

"If you want it enough. If you develop a bit of Rosie's determination and don't let anything get in your way. If you don't let your weaknesses trap you..."

A great star! "Do you really, truly think so, Mr. Morgan?"

He didn't answer; his head had dropped forward and his breath came with faint snores.

Deirdre studied him in his sleep. Relaxed, his cheeks sagged. There was a net of deep wrinkles around his eyes and mouth. He didn't look at all like Charlie Morgan, the song-and-dance man twirling his cane and tilting his straw hat. Without greasepaint, he was an old man. But maybe he knew about stars. And that wonderful audience back in Topeka—maybe they knew, too.

TWENTY-ONE

They were in the last town before Denver. The last show was over, Deirdre had late supper with the Santinis at the soda fountain across from the hotel, and they were all going upstairs. But Mrs. Santini held Deirdre back.

"Wait, hon. I need to talk to you."

There was a rickety swing on the porch of the hotel. Mrs. Santini led Deirdre to it. They sat side by side. Mrs. Santini put her arm around Deirdre's shoulders.

"I don't know how to say this," Mrs. Santini said.

Deirdre felt a funny tingle at the base of her spine.

"The act's not working. Deirdre, you're too unhappy, and it shows. It doesn't work."

The swing creaked as Mrs. Santini shifted her weight. "We have to give Marie your part in Denver."

"But—but you need Marie in back, tumbling and—"

"I know, it's temporary. Mr. Bremer's coming to the show in Denver. It'll be better with Marie. He'll make allowances because he understands we're short-handed, and—we need to get booked for next year, Deirdre. We need to. Bremer's bringing someone to Denver to replace—um, Tina. So she'll be trained and ready to go for the next stop."

Deirdre stared out into the dark. Clouds drifted across the half-moon.

"Deirdre, everyone knows you're talented; you're just not right for the act. I'm so sorry. It's business, hon."

What would she do now? She'd almost made it to Texas. What could she do now?

"In Denver, we'll put you on a train back to Greenville; you'll have to change trains, but we'll alert the conductor, so don't worry. We'll take care of everything. We'll make sure you get home safe and sound. This is really hard for me. You're a lovely girl, and I know you tried, but—"

She'd have to run again. Texas was so far, so far to go all alone. Deirdre began to shiver.

"I bet you've missed your mom and dad. It'll be good for you to be home again, and they'll be so happy to have you back."

"Please, let me stay with you until Texas," Deirdre whispered. "Please, let me travel with the show just to Texas. I don't have to be in it, that's okay."

"Well, no, Texas is just that much further from Greenville, there's no point—Denver's the best connection."

What if Sean came looking for her at a theater in Texas and she couldn't get there in time?... She had to, that's all. Traveling all alone. It was so hard. Too hard.

"I'm so sorry," Mrs. Santini said. "You know, you're

awfully young to be away from your family. You'll see, you'll be glad to be home again."

"The troupe feels like family," Deirdre whispered through the terrible thickening in her throat.

"I suppose," Mrs. Santini said. "Vaudeville can be a string of lonely train rides and lonely hotels. So we're close on the road. But, you know, at the end of a tour, people get different bookings and go their separate ways. Another tour, a new group forms. For the time that we're together, it is a sort of family, but, Deirdre, your blood family is permanent. Your own mother and—"

Deirdre was glad it was dark. She was glad Mrs. Santini couldn't see her face.

Deirdre wished she could tell her the truth. Instead, she begged, "I could help one of the other acts. Or—or walk the poodles. Or…or—"

"Don't, hon." Mrs. Santini rose. "Let's go upstairs. You'll get a good night's rest, and in the morning, you'll see it's for the best…"

Deirdre hugged herself and shivered. "I—I want to stay down here for a while."

Deirdre held her tears back until she heard the screen door slam. Then she dropped her head and sobbed. And knew that all the crying in the world wouldn't change a thing. It never had. She'd run as soon as they arrived in Denver.

Everyone at breakfast the next morning knew what had happened.

"Gee, kid, that's too bad," Trixie Dee said.

"I'm awfully sorry." Rosie's eyes over her coffee cup were sympathetic. She lowered her voice. "What are you going to do now?"

Deirdre shook her head. "I don't know."

"You'll get away from all this craziness, that's what," Maxie said. "Show business ain't no life for a kid."

"Wait a minute," Charlie Morgan said. "There has to be something we could—"

"The Santinis won't change their minds," Deirdre said. "I begged Mrs. Santini, but—"

"Well, they've got to think of the act," Gloria said.

"You never belonged in that act in the first place," Charlie Morgan interrupted. "A colossal waste of talent."

"That's the truth," Rosie put in. "Deirdre wowed 'em in Topeka."

"I didn't think you'd watch me in Topeka," Deirdre said, "because you always turn inward before your—"

"Yeah, but I could feel something happening out front," Rosie said. "The way that audience—"

"Never saw anything like it. Why can't she have a spot of her own?" Charlie Morgan asked. "Any good reason?"

"A spot of my own?" Deirdre felt a nervous, thrilled tingle crawl up her back.

"The kid deserves a break," Trixie Dee said, "but not without Bremer's say-so. He don't run auditions on the road."

"He's meeting up with us in Denver, isn't he?" Charlie said. "He could check her out in the matinee."

"You mean have her audition on stage, in *performance?*" Gloria said. "He'll never go for that!"

"I'll call him right now," Charlie said. He threw down his napkin. "Listen, he knows I played the Palace, he knows my judgment is gold."

"Mr. Show Business in person," Trixie muttered.

"I can sell him on Deirdre," Charlie said. "Charlie Morgan still has clout." He drew himself up as he left the table to find a telephone.

Deirdre was afraid to hope too much. She couldn't breathe.

Rosie gave her a hard look. "The old man's putting himself on the line for you."

That made Deirdre cringe. She was planning to take off in Texas! How could she have forgotten? Would that get Charlie Morgan in trouble? No sense in thinking about that, most probably Mr. Bremer wouldn't listen to Mr. Morgan anyway...

It was the longest morning of Deirdre's life. Charlie Morgan couldn't reach Mr. Bremer on the first try. He left a message. Deirdre waited and waited at the front desk of the rooming house. Mr. Bremer didn't call back. Finally, Charlie phoned again.

Mr. Bremer agreed to see her perform! She'd have a five-minute spot of her own, squeezed in between Trixie Dee and the Great Regurgitator. In Denver, it wouldn't be 9 WORLD FAMOUS ACTS 9. It would be 10!

"Deirdre, remember, this is only for the matinee," Mr.

Morgan warned. "Anything could happen—maybe Bremer will have indigestion or a fight with his wife. This doesn't mean you're in."

Deirdre nodded.

"Don't count on much," Trixie added.

"No, I won't." But she couldn't help it; this was the only thing left to count on.

"I'm so happy you'll get a chance, hon." Mrs. Santini gave her a quick hug.

"But—but I don't have an act," Deirdre said. They had only a day of traveling before Denver!

"Not enough time to work something up," Mr. Santini said. "Choose a song you know and keep it simple."

"I have a dress for you," Gloria said. "It doesn't fit anymore; I held on to it in case I lost those ten pounds."

"There won't be time for a run-through with the band," Mrs. Santini said. "See if the musicians will go over your song on the train."

"They will." Rosie grinned. "I have pull with the trumpet section."

The songs she used to sing on the street raced through Deirdre's mind. "I Found a Million-Dollar Baby in a Five and Ten Cent Store," "Bye, Bye, Blackbird"… "'Danny Boy'?" she asked. "'Peg o' My Heart'?"

"Forget it, no Irish songs," Rosie said harshly. "I'm the colleen act, remember?"

Deirdre, startled, mumbled, "I'm sorry." She didn't mean to step on Rosie's toes! Okay, no Irish songs. "'Let a Smile Be

Your Umbrella,' 'April Showers'…I know! 'There'll Be Some Changes Made.'" She remembered how strong that song had made her feel back at the Gansworthys. She could belt it!

"Not bad. Upbeat," Mr. Morgan said. "Keep 'em smiling!"

"You've got to slow it way down, though," Mr. Santini said. "There has to be a slow song right after Trixie's number."

"Let's see the dress, Gloria," Mrs. Santini said.

The dress was white cotton eyelet. It was so pretty, but it was way too big and too long.

"What'll I wear?" Deirdre moaned. Hadn't Mr. Morgan told her an actor always dressed proud, with spotless shirt, shoes polished to a high shine, no run-down heels ever? Even if it took your last dime. But everything she had was second-hand and shabby!

"Don't worry, I can do something with it." Mrs. Santini sighed. "I wish I had my sewing machine."

"Yeah, Ma, and how would we carry it?" Vincent said.

"I get so tired of traveling light…Well, I'd better get busy."

"White's a good stage color; it draws the light," Rosie said. "And you'll look beautiful with your dark hair and—" Then she frowned. "But you should change your name. We don't want them expecting an Irish act, do we?"

Deirdre's lips set into a stubborn line. "No, I'm keeping my name!" Because it's mine, she thought. Because if I become a famous star, I want everyone to know! Norma and

Miss Harrow and Mrs. Gansworthy and everyone who's ever been mean to me. The Gansworthys! No, she wouldn't let herself be afraid anymore. If she became a big star, they couldn't touch her. And Mum—Mum would be proud. Wait—what was she thinking? She was quitting show business in Texas.

"Come on, folks," Maxie yelled. "We better make that train!"

On the train, Gloria cut the dress and Mrs. Santini hand-sewed. Across the aisle, Gene and the piano player went over the tempo with Deirdre.

"I know Mr. Santini said—but it's supposed to be a fast, finger-snapping song. Isn't it?" Deirdre asked.

"It'll work," Gene said. "Nice and slow, show off that vibrato you've got. I'll bring the trumpet in under you and—remember the way we did 'Silent Night'?"

"We'll make you sound great," the piano player said. "Now let's go over the…"

All these people were working so hard to help her, Deirdre thought, and she would have to run off in Texas without even saying good-bye. And Charlie Morgan had put himself on the line for her! She'd have to be wonderful in Denver so Mr. Bremer would still trust his judgment. But she'd be letting Charlie Morgan down. How could she do that? She would—for Sean. Sean, her blood brother. But it made her feel terrible.

TWENTY-TWO

The Royal wasn't really in Denver. There was a beautiful theater in the heart of the city, Mr. Morgan said, with gold molding and separate big, clean dressing rooms for the men and the women. But that theater booked only the top troupes on the Keith and Orpheum circuits.

The Royal was way past city limits. It was an old wooden building. As the audience came in, Deirdre could hear boots stamping on the plank floor.

"Looks like a bunch of roughneck miners and loggers," Maxie reported. "Watch out for tomatoes!"

"What?" Deirdre asked nervously.

"He's only kidding," Rosie said.

"No, he's not," Trixie put in.

Up until now, Deirdre had kept her mind on her dress and her song and getting her makeup on. Suddenly a new realization panicked her. She'd be on the stage all alone. Without the Santinis to carry the act. By herself, with no one to depend on! And Mr. Bremer was out front somewhere!

"Where's the hoochy-koochy girls?" a husky voice brayed.

Her stomach flipped over and Deirdre clutched Rosie's sleeve. "I feel sick. I'm going to throw up!"

"What? You wanna steal the Great Regurgitator's act now?" Rosie said.

"I mean it," Deirdre moaned. "I can't do this. All those roughnecks out front!"

"Listen, Deirdre." Rosie grasped her by the shoulders and looked straight into her eyes. "Listen to me. If they could do half of what we can, they'd be on the stage. But they can't. That's why *we're* on the stage and *they're* in the seats. And you'll go out there and show them!"

The Ping Brothers were on. Feet were still stamping in. "We want the hoochy-koochies!"

This is terrible, Deirdre thought. The Ping Brothers do such difficult tricks and work so hard to perfect them!

Deirdre's breath was coming too fast, and she couldn't slow it down. How would she manage to sing? "There'll Be Some Changes Made"—it was supposed to be a finger-snapping, energetic song, and she had to sing it slow! Why did she ever pick that one?

Trixie Dee, the tinny sound of her ukulele. A big laugh when she fell on her hula-hula behind. Trixie was almost through.

Deirdre was on next. She stood in the wings, paralyzed with fear. "Bend your knees," Rosie whispered. "Stretch. Loosen up."

"…and now the little girl with the great big voice, DEIRDRE O'ROURKE!"

"We want women!" someone yelled out. "Bring on the nekkid women!"

There was a moment of hush when Deirdre came on stage. There was always that hush, just a second, when even the rowdy audiences were curious and gave you a chance. And you had to grab them right then and there, or you lost them.

The band played the intro. The spotlight shone on Deirdre.

"There's a change in the weather, there's a change in the
    sea…
So from now on there'll be a change in me…"

If Bremer didn't like her… Running to Texas all alone… Nothing had changed. All she had was hope. She bent the note, let the yearning make her voice sob… And the saxophone moaned behind her.

"Nobody wants you when you're old and gray…"

Or young and poor, she thought. She dragged the notes into a dark bluesy sound. She, Sean, Jimmy, sad cross-eyed Aloysius, abandoned and unwanted. What could ever fix that?

"There'll be some changes made today…"

Her voice was dipping and tailing, raw hope against hopelessness. She and Sean hadn't managed back home. It would take some huge changes to survive on the run. A new start. Somehow, someway, she'd make it work... They were quiet, they were listening. They were listening!

"There'll be some changes made..."

Like a prayer from the bottom of her soul. Singing for her life.

She had them! They were breathing with her, electricity passing from her to them and back again. Maybe they knew what it was like to live on just a tiny sliver of hope; they were wrapping a protective blanket of love around her! Now she could do anything!

In the second chorus, she strutted across the stage, a pointed gesture with each word, believing in herself, singing her heart out, letting go with everything she had, and Gene's trumpet weaving around her, egging her on to reach higher and higher.

"My walk will be different and my talk and my name, Nothin' about me is going to be the same..."

No, she'd never let anyone give her a new name, like poor Peg, to suit someone else! She held her head high, feeling the power, feeling brave and tall, believing. She was *somebody!*

"I'm going to change my way of living and if that ain't
    enough
I'll even change the way I strut my stuff…"

And on to the last lines, her eyes welling up with
jumbled emotion, she wanted, she wanted so much!

"There'll be some changes made today
Oh, yeah! There'll be some changes made!"

Everything was coming together, this was where she
belonged, right here, voice soaring, tears shining in her eyes,
she'd done it!

And then—stamping, whistles, applause, sweet applause.
One more call, they didn't want to let her off, and then she
was running, running into the wings.

"…a tough act to follow," the Regurgitator muttered.

"Not a dry eye in the house," Mr. Morgan said.

And Deirdre was sweating and laughing and almost
crying. All that love, all that love flowing to her. It was all
she'd ever wanted. She had to be in that spotlight again.
And again. And again!

At intermission, Mr. Bremer came backstage. "Where's
O'Rourke?"

"Here, Mr. Bremer." Deirdre held her breath while he
looked at her with shrewd, narrowed eyes.

"Not bad, kid." He had a harsh voice and a rough way
of talking. "Not too bad."

What did that mean?

"Tell you what. Get a second song ready. You have a ten-minute spot like all the others. No more, got that? Ten minutes and don't milk it, keep it movin'!" He scowled as he chomped on his cigar, but Deirdre was too aglow to be scared of him.

He was even going to pay her! Later, everyone said he'd shortchanged her, but she was dizzy with joy. Money of her own, and for singing on the stage! She couldn't wait to do it again.

Deirdre rested beside Rosie in the dressing room. Rosie was leaning toward the mirror, removing her makeup between shows.

Deirdre watched her peeling off the false eyelashes. "I don't know where you get the patience." Putting on stage makeup had seemed so strange and exciting just a short while ago. It had turned into a constant monotonous chore.

Rosie spread thick gobs of cream over the greasepaint. "Well, you sure killed them. You *murdered* them!"

"I was so scared and then it felt so good. And Mr. Bremer's letting me have a second song! I wish I knew how to dance, maybe do some steps in between."

"Charlie could show you." Rosie was busy tissuing off. "Naw, you don't need anything else. You've got the voice, that's enough."

"I like your big finish with the dance. I always wondered, though, why the cancan? I mean, in a colleen act?"

"Well, an Irish jig wouldn't show much leg, would it?" Rosie laughed. "Listen, my legs are most of my act."

"Don't say that. You can sing and dance so great and—"

"Thanks, but I know the truth. I wish I'd had real dance training," Rosie said. "I used to sneak in the vaudeville houses through the fire door and pick up whatever—"

Deirdre grinned. "You, too? I knew we had a connection."

"You learned to dance by watching and—"

"No. I meant the fire door."

"That's how I picked up the cancan. It sure got them today. That was some house, wasn't it? I didn't think they'd ever let me off!" Rosie gazed at her reflection. "Did you hear them stamping and carrying on? I had them right in the palm of my hand. If 'Family Fare' Bremer wasn't out front, I'd have given them a shimmy. They'd eat up a shimmy! They loved me!"

I have exactly the same fever Rosie has, Deirdre thought.

"What about you?" Rosie raised an eyebrow. "After that performance—you're still going off with your brother?"

"Yes, of course. That's why I came…" Deirdre's voice trailed off. "You come to the end of the line in Texas anyway."

"The end of the line going west," Rosie corrected. "A couple of days in Galveston, and then we take the southern route going east till we wind up back in New York."

"Oh." They'd go on from theater to theater, hotel to

hotel, and she wouldn't be there. Trixie and Mr. Morgan and the Santinis and Rosie and—they'd all go on without her. And her space between Trixie Dee and the Great Regurgitator would close up as if she'd never held it at all.

"I feel bad about Charlie Morgan," Deirdre said. "Will Mr. Bremer be mad at him on account of me?"

"You're going to leave Charlie looking foolish," Rosie said, "but don't worry about Bremer. Charlie's still an attraction, at least for Allstate." She glanced sideways at Deirdre. "Don't tell anyone, but I've been talking to someone from the Orpheum circuit. I think I can work out a switch pretty soon. Anyway, I'm hoping."

"What about Gene?" Deirdre asked.

"What about him?"

"Will he go with the Orpheum, too?"

"No, I guess he'll stay with the band. Wherever they go. He's not that ambitious." Rosie pulled her glorious hair back and studied herself in the mirror. "God, the Orpheum circuit! That's a different world."

"But Gene—I thought you were in *love* with him."

"I could be. I'll miss him something awful, I know that."

"And you'd leave him anyway?" Deirdre asked. Maybe everything Charlie Morgan had said about Rosie was true.

"You disapprove?" Rosie snapped. "You don't know how much I gave up to get this far. I'm the disgrace of my family. I've never even seen my baby brother. Well, I gave up too much to let anything or anyone stop me now!"

185

"Your family? Aren't they proud of—"

"You don't understand. They're religious, with the old-country ways. My sister was the good one; she went to work in the sweatshops, and I saw all the life drain out of her. Not me, I thought, not me!"

"What happened? What did they—"

"No, no more." Rosie slammed the jar of cold cream on the counter. "From now on, I'm keeping my mind on the Orpheum circuit. Hey, Palace, here I come!"

"The Palace," Deirdre breathed. Maybe Rosie would really make it. Maybe she could, too, if— Well, she'd never know.

Rosie stretched and met Deirdre's eyes in the mirror. "So you're not the least bit stagestruck? You've got to be after that performance!" She smiled. "Could be that's another connection we have."

Deirdre shrugged. Of course she was! She was as stagestruck as if she'd been hit by lightning! But seeing Sean again—that was the impossible dream that might be about to come true. Sean. Her brother.

"Just asking," Rosie said.

I like Rosie, Deirdre thought. She couldn't really blame Rosie for the times she'd been distant. Rosie could be fun and friendly, but she looked out for herself. Maybe she hadn't wanted a clingy twelve-year-old always tagging after her. And that, Deirdre thought, is exactly what I've been—clingy and needy. Well, she'd changed. When she and Sean were together again, he'd see her taking on an equal share of whatever troubles faced them. He'd be surprised by how much she'd grown up! But she'd miss the talk about circuits and spots, and the backstage gossip...What would Charlie Morgan think of her after she was gone? She'd miss the long train rides with everyone together. New towns, new theaters, checking out new audiences. It would be hard to walk away!

Maybe—maybe Sean could join the show...But he didn't sing. Or dance. Or anything. And she wasn't sure he'd fit in. He'd think Mr. Morgan's way of talking was too uppity...

No, they'd take off together. She didn't know how they'd manage on their own, but she wouldn't leave Sean stuck alone someplace in Texas. She wasn't as tough as Rosie. She'd stand by him. The way he'd always stood by her.

TWENTY-THREE

They played two more Colorado towns. Deirdre added "Amazing Grace"; that and "There'll Be Some Changes Made" got them every time! When she was on stage, she felt as if she carried a radiant light of her own inside, shining as powerfully as any spotlight.

From the wings, she watched the new girl in the Santinis' act. Her name was June. She sang the Napoli song with a dumb, bored expression on her face, and when she reached for the high C and just missed it, she put on a smug look as if she was so proud of herself. It was *funny!* Off stage, June wasn't dumb at all. She was acting, working it as a comedienne, and the Six Santinis went over great. I wasn't too good for the Six Santinis, Deirdre thought, embarrassed, I wasn't good enough! Maybe she'd catch Maxie or Shane in a serious moment and ask them about comic timing, just to know...

Deirdre was learning the craft. Like the others, she worked on perfecting every gesture. Every little move counted.

The troupe had been nice to her before; they'd considered her a good kid and treated her like one of them. But now she was getting respect as an equal. Deirdre was proud that she earned it, every day and every night, in the applause that came for her with each show.

She knew they wouldn't care that she'd come off an orphan train. Talent, pure and simple, was the only thing that mattered to vaudeville people. Rich, poor, where you came from, or who your folks were didn't count. It seemed to Deirdre that this was far more fair than the way she'd been judged in the world outside.

In the morning, they rode out of Colorado. Marie looked out of the train window at a picture-book house in the distance, smoke curling out of its chimney. "It must be nice to live in the same cozy house all the time and have your friends there and go to regular school…" she said wistfully.

Deirdre knew what was inside some of those houses. She was so glad that she'd escaped the old man's room at the Andersons' and the gloom of the Gansworthys' dining room. And now they were crossing the border into Texas!

"The Texas Panhandle," Mr. Santini said.

Deirdre saw flat land, not a tree in sight, frosted brown prairie grass. Once in a while, there was an oil derrick in the distance. Texas! She was actually here!

Deirdre was too excited to sit still. She went up the aisle of the train, asking, "Does anybody have a map of Texas?"

"Not me," Trixie said. "You think I'd lug an atlas along?"

"No," the Great Regurgitator said. "What do you need it for?"

"Our first show is Fort Worth, that's all I know," the unicycle boy said.

"I was just wondering," Deirdre said. "Is Bandera near Fort Worth?"

"Bandera? Never heard of it."

Charlie Morgan was sitting in front of the Great Regurgitator. Deirdre had been avoiding him; she felt uncomfortable around him now. But he was listening to her questions with a look of interest.

"I know Bandera's close to Austin," she said to him. "Is that anywhere near Fort Worth?"

"No, it's another part of the state. Texas is the largest in the U.S., you know."

"Which is Austin closest to? Fort Worth, Houston, or Galveston?"

"Houston, I guess," Charlie Morgan said. "Why do you ask?"

"No reason, just wondering," Deirdre said as guilt washed over her.

Then Sean wouldn't be coming to Fort Worth. But they'd be in Houston in a couple of days. Soon. She would see Sean soon! Against all odds, they wouldn't lose each other! Just the thought put a sparkle in her eyes. And for the matinee in Fort Worth, she sang "There'll Be Some Changes Made" like the optimistic song it was meant to be. She was feeling so good—for the last verse she took a chance and signaled the band to pick up the tempo. Playfully, she growled an imitation of Sophie Tucker, red-hot-mama style. They loved it! Even the band applauded!

Fort Worth was two shows a day. There was time to kill before the evening performance. Some people went back to the rooming house. In the dressing room, Deirdre changed into Trixie's old kimono. She tilted back in a chair and rested her feet on a crate. Lou Ping came in with their food orders in a brown paper bag. "Who gets the jelly doughnut? Who gets coffee with cream, coffee black…"

"American cheese on white is mine," Deirdre said.

Lou handed it to her and said, "There's some rube outside asking for you. A young guy."

"For me?" The sandwich dropped from her suddenly useless hands. Could it be Sean? Could Sean have hitched all the way to Fort Worth?

She raced down the stairs, looping the sash as she ran. She opened the stage door and squinted into the sudden flood of sunlight. And—Sean!

"Sean!" She ran to him, flew into his hug. Something felt strange—they were on eye level, that was it, she'd suddenly become as tall as him. "Oh, Sean!"

"Hey, little sister." He released her, and they stepped back, awkwardly examining each other, smiling and smiling with shaky lips.

He looked different, almost unfamiliar. He'd filled out so much. He wasn't skinny anymore. Her Sean! He had a tan, with sunburn on his nose; she was used to his skin fair and pale. His hair was different. But the big change was in something else…His expression. His posture. The tough, wary look was gone.

"I saw the show," he said. "You were great. I didn't know you could…I knew you could sing, but…The way you were…I had to keep telling myself it was you. You weren't scared or nothing in front of all—"

"You saw me? I didn't even know you were here! I thought Houston—" She couldn't stop staring at him. Finally, Sean—and it wasn't just a dream!

"I couldn't wait." He grinned. He looked her over. "Deirdre—what's that you're wearing?"

She glanced down. "Oh. Trixie's kimono. I borrow it between shows so my dress won't—"

"You're half undressed. And made-up like—Trixie's the fat one does the hula? You're friends with her?"

"Trixie's nice. I know she looks a little—" Self-consciously, Deirdre tied her sash tighter. "But when you get to know her, she's nice."

"It don't matter." He smiled. "You're finished with all that now."

"I guess so," she said uncertainly.

"If I'd known how bad it was in Greenville…You should've told me sooner. Why didn't you tell me?"

"You couldn't have done anything. Anyway, that's over."

"But I feel so bad that you— Yeah, you're right, that's over. Wait till you see the ranch!" His smile was open and boyish. "Well, it's not much of a spread, kind of hard-scrabble, but—I'm good with horses, real good, horses are smart and sensitive, did you know that, and we're breeding mustangs with Thoroughbreds. Well, you'll see. The Langfords are the best, you'll love them!"

"The Langfords?" What does he mean? Deirdre thought. I won't be seeing them, we're running off together, aren't we?

"Lorene's gonna love having a girl around. I got two older brothers, did I tell you? They're grown and married, but they come over pretty regular. They're great. With all those boys, Lorene's itching to sew up some ruffly pinafores."

"What?"

"You'll meet Roy and Lorene in a minute. They're wait-ing at the soda fountain down the street. They thought we'd want some time by ourselves first before we—"

"The Langfords, *here?* I don't understand. What—?"

He laughed. "I got so much to tell you, I'm telling it all mixed up. The Langfords—we hit it off from the begin-ning. Well, no, the first couple of days were rocky, I was gonna run, see, I wasn't used to anyone telling me what to do. And then we had a talk over breakfast—wait till you taste Pop's blueberry pancakes!—we had a talk and I saw they'd say exactly what was on their minds, straight out, and I started to trust them. Gee, that seems so long ago. The thing is—the Langfords love me. And I call them Mom and Pop now." For a moment, Deirdre saw a trace of the familiar defiant look. "I love Lorene and I call her Mom. Because Mum gave us up. I don't owe her nothing."

"You were the one always defending her," Deirdre said.

"I know. Because I blamed myself, not her. I was supposed to be the man in the family, I was supposed to take care of everybody, you, Jimmy, and Mum. I was always thinking I failed her. See, with Lorene, I found out what a mother's supposed to be like. Lorene takes care of me. I mean, not that I need care, but— And you know something? Giving us away was no small thing. It was no small thing!"

That's true, Deirdre thought. All these months, she'd watched the Santinis and she was as sure as anything that Mrs. Santini would never give away Marie, Vincent, or Carl, no matter what happened. She'd fight like a tiger for them.

"I don't think Mum did right," Deirdre said slowly, "but I think it was hard for her."

"No. No excuse for what she did to us."

"She had some kind of reason. Maybe she thought we'd be better off. I won't look for her," Deirdre said, "but if I ever see her again, I think I'll forgive her."

"But you were the one got the worst of it! Well, it'll be different now. I'm the Langfords' son, they're adopting me legal, and they'll take you in, too, 'cause you're my sister. They'll love you, too, I know they will. You'll get used to Pop's rules."

What would she do on a ranch with "Pop's rules"?

"'Cause they're fair; everyone has to pull their own weight and be responsible," Sean continued. "Like school-work—I go every day, that's my job, see, and I'm doing good. And if you're taking care of the horses, you can't slough it off; you go out to the stable even if it's pouring rain, and…It's home, Deirdre. The best place I ever been."

"I thought—I thought you'd be hitching here and then we'd take off and maybe snatch Jimmy and run back east and—"

"Jimmy on the *run?*" Sean said. "Don't worry, Jimmy's in a good place. I told you I been writing to his folks. I thought about asking the Langfords if I could get him, but it wouldn't be right to take him away. Jimmy's attached and happy; it wouldn't be right to move him again. His folks write me all the cute things he does and how smart he is— you can tell he's the apple of their eye. It's you I feel bad about, the time you spent in Greenville… well, you're with me now. You don't have to travel with those showpeople anymore."

"I like them," Deirdre said.

"It was a long way for you to come—I was worried. Going from place to place like that, Lord knows what kind of places."

"I liked being on the road," Deirdre said. "I learned a lot. You won't believe all the things I know! Listen, Sean, I know how to hold an audience, you can't always depend on it happening by accident, I know all the tricks and…I'm good, Sean. Everyone says so. Right now I'm on between

Trixie Dee and the Regurgitator, but if it wasn't for Rosie France, I bet I'd get last spot before intermission. That's almost as good as the star spot, 'cause you got to bring them back after intermission...I have so much to tell you! Michael—he's the piano player—Michael's teaching me to read music! All those funny little squiggles mean different sounds, and I'm catching on. You have to meet Rosie France! Oh, and I want to tell you about Mr. Morgan, he's the song-and-dance man, he played the Palace with Eddie Cantor and—"

Deirdre stopped for breath, and she caught Sean studying her.

"You sound happy about it," Sean said. "Like it wasn't that bad."

"I like it. A lot."

Deirdre looked into the deep blue of Sean's eyes, the only thing that hadn't changed. That, and the way he had his thumb hooked into his pocket... For a moment, she saw the Sean that used to be. The way he looked now, she thought, was the way he would have been from the very beginning if he'd had enough food and sunshine and didn't have to be so defensive.

"You're happy, too," Deirdre said.

"Well, yeah, sure," Sean answered. "Listen, we ought to meet up with the Langfords and get started; we got a long way to go. Where are your things?"

"Back at the rooming house," Deirdre answered. And she imagined herself packing up and going off with people she didn't know yet, good people who'd take her in because of their love for Sean. She'd be leaving her vaudeville family behind. Even if it wasn't exactly a family, there was the bond as they sat side by side putting on the greasepaint every day, gossiping, grousing, and then sharing that thrilled flutter when they heard "Five minutes." She'd never get to learn the buck and wing from Mr. Morgan. She'd never again laugh herself sick at Maxie and Shane's crazy stunts. She'd never hear if Rosie managed to get herself into the Orpheum. Michael was just about to explain sharps and flats to her. The Santinis and little Marie and... But—another tour, different bookings, and a new group would form. She understood that. So the thought of leaving them shouldn't be hurting so much or making her throat feel tight. She was lucky. She'd just found her real family, her blood brother Sean.

"Come on." Sean tugged at her. "We have to get your stuff and—"

Deirdre took a few steps with him and then stopped short. "I can't go now. There's a show tonight. We have to stay until after the show."

Sean frowned. "Bandera's a long way. Gotta feed the livestock and—all we've got is a horse and wagon, I told you we ain't rich, and it's a long way."

"I have a show to do!"

"So tell them you can't make it. It can go on without you, can't it? What's the difference?"

They were still billed as 9 WORLD FAMOUS ACTS 9; the

sign hadn't been changed yet. The Great Regurgitator could go on after Trixie Dee, the way it was before. But— but she *wanted* to do the show. Her last one. And then it hit her. It couldn't be her last, it couldn't!

"Come on," Sean said, pulling her along. The way he used to. When she was a scared little girl who needed him to direct her. "Come on, it's late. We got to get started... When you first see the ranch—well, February's not the prettiest month out here. But Lorene says wait till you see it in springtime, with the fields full of bluebonnets."

What did she care about bluebonnets? She wanted to stand in the wings, turning inward, gathering herself, gathering the power that would explode on stage. The spotlight and the hush. And then the audience's love washing over her, the applause and the afterglow. It was the stage that she couldn't leave!

"Sean, wait," Deirdre said. She could hardly get the words out. "Sean, I can't."

Sean turned back. "Can't what?"

"I can't go with you. I can't give it up," she whispered. "I thought I could, but—I can't."

"You don't want to come with me?" Sean searched her face for a long time. "You're that happy in vaudeville?"

"I am. I love it. More than I've ever loved anything."

"Are you sure? You don't have to—"

"I'm sure."

"Just riding around on one train and another? That don't sound good. Who's taking care of you? And—and what about school? You're supposed to be in school."

"Well, I guess the Santinis are still kind of in charge of me, on this tour anyway. Mrs. Santini makes me do lessons on the train. I know my times tables and—"

"I was planning on you coming home with me."

"It's all right, honest. I can take care of myself."

"But what about—"

"And I'm not alone. Everyone looks out for everyone else."

"The Langfords are all ready to—you didn't even meet them yet. Why don't you wait until you meet them and then— I'm telling you, they're great, don't be scared, they'll—"

"I'm not scared. Sean, listen to me. I have something I can do better than anybody. Something that's all mine. And a place where I belong. Really and truly belong. Sean, I can't leave it. I can't."

After a long while, Sean nodded. "I guess I know how that is," he said. "I found my place, too."

"It's good that we both did," Deirdre said. "And Jimmy, too."

"I know," Sean said. "I wish it could be the same place. Together."

Tears began to well up in Deirdre's eyes. "All those months, all I thought about was finding you again. That's all I thought about. How much I missed you and— But I can't—"

Sean put his arm around her. "It's okay, Deirdre. We found each other, didn't we? It's okay."

Deirdre nodded. "We'll always be family, won't we? You, me, and Jimmy."

"We're family. Nothing can change that." Sean blinked hard; his eyes looked shiny—wet. "The three of us. Wherever we are."

"You, me, and Jimmy," Deirdre whispered. "You'll get Jimmy's address to me, okay?"

"Okay. He can't write yet, but his folks will— Listen, if it don't work out for you, you know I'm here. Remember that."

"And—and the show will be in Texas awhile. Maybe you could come see me again in Houston—and Galveston?"

"Houston for sure," Sean said.

They stood together in silence, near each other, quiet, not quite touching, holding on to the last minutes of being together. Deirdre knew he had to go. And she had to get ready for a performance. She memorized his face, this new face that wasn't afraid to be unguarded or show his feelings.

"We won't lose each other, not ever," Deirdre whispered. "I bet there'll be lots of other tours going through Texas. You'll always come to my shows, won't you?"

"Wild horses couldn't keep me away," he said. "And in between we'll write and—" He rubbed a trail of mascara off her cheek. He put a hand on each side of her face and held it, looking into her eyes. "Are you going to be okay, Deirdre?"

"I know I will be." Deirdre smiled through her tears.

"So no good-bye," Sean said. "Just—next time."

"Next time," Deirdre repeated. She watched him walk down the sidewalk. He turned to give her a little wave. Then he disappeared around the corner. It was just like that terrible time when she'd been taken away in Greenville! They'd never said good-bye then, either. The memory was unbearable. She almost ran after him—quick, before it's too late, she thought—but she couldn't move.

She wiped her eyes. Her makeup was a mess! She rushed back to the dressing room to redo it.

"Five minutes!"

She beaded fresh mascara and thought, I'm giving up being Sean's day-in and day-out sister, growing up with him. Still family, but it won't be the same. How can I do that?

She could hear the Ping Brothers on stage. A smattering of applause for their hoop routine.

Sean would be coming to Houston. She'd have another chance to go home with him... But she knew she wouldn't.

A drumroll. That meant the Pings were throwing the flaming clubs.

Had she turned as tough as Rosie? Maybe that wasn't all bad. Maybe that's what it took to *choose* instead of letting herself get blown about by the wind. If Rosie left, maybe she'd ask Mr. Bremer for the before-intermission spot. Deirdre remembered Mr. Morgan's words. "A star... if you want it enough... if you don't let anything get in your way." *Yes, she wanted it enough!* The thought was terrifying and thrilling at the same time.

"Deirdre!" someone called. "Hurry, Trixie's on!"

She rushed into position on the stage-right side. It was a full house. Trixie Dee and "Hannah does the hula-ha, hula-ha, hula-ha..." Waiting in the wings. The ukulele plinking the tune. Waiting, hardly breathing. How she loved this, how she loved all of it! A good hand for Trixie...

"...that little girl with the great big voice, DEIRDRE O'ROURKE!"

Into the spotlight. The expectant hush. "There'll Be Some Changes Made."

The applause, the whistles, waves of love coming at her, that delicious warm golden glow. Then the opening chords of "Amazing Grace."

"Amazing Grace, how sweet the sound," she sang, "that saved a wretch like me," with the trumpet coming in on a piercing high note of triumph.

When I caught that midnight train out of Greenville, Deirdre thought, I never imagined it would bring me so far!

"I once was lost but now am found..." she sang, and her heart spilled over with joy and gratitude. For she would never be lost again. Here, behind the footlights, right here, she had found her home at last.

Afterword

In the 1800s and early 1900s, waves of immigrants came to American cities to escape famine or persecution in their home countries. On New York City's Lower East Side, mostly Irish, Italians, and Jews were packed into airless, crowded tenements or makeshift shelters, where they lived in extreme poverty. Under those miserable conditions, diseases spread quickly, making orphans of many children. Other children were placed in orphanages by parents who could no longer feed or care for them. Some children were simply abandoned and survived on the streets as best they could, often as petty thieves.

The sight of so many pathetic waifs inspired Charles Loring Brace to help by starting the Children's Aid Society in 1853. It was his idea to give children from the teeming city streets and orphanages a chance at adoption in rural communities. They were bathed, dressed in new clothes, and sent out by train for new and better lives. Brace believed the children needed to make a clean break with the past. No keepsakes were permitted. Parents and children could not keep track of each other, though siblings adopted separately were allowed to keep in touch.

From a very few up to three hundred children, babies through age fourteen, went on each train. Agents from the

Children's Aid Society took care of them on the way. The trips could last a few days or several weeks.

Crowds of people waited at each stop. Some planned to adopt, and some came just for the entertainment of watching children being chosen. Many children were welcomed into happy new families. Others were mistreated and used as farm laborers or maids. Their stories and experiences were as different as the more than one hundred thousand individual children who rode the trains between 1854 and 1930.

By 1930, there were new programs to help children and immigrants and new laws to control adoption. The orphan trains came to an end.